THE
AVIATOR
CRAIG DILOUIE

THE AVIATOR

Cover art and layout by EK Cover Design.

Published by ZING Communications, Inc.

www.CraigDiLouie.com

TECHNICAL NOTE & ACKNOWLEDGMENTS

To create a realistic and gritty story of near-future warfare in the Pacific, every effort was taken to capture what it might be like to fight in an F/A-18 Super Hornet squadron against the People's Republic of China (PRC). Sources and inspiration included a variety of websites, manuals, and books such as *Another Great Day at Sea* by Geoff Dyer, *Carrier* by Tom Clancy, and *Jet Girl* by Caroline Johnson.

I owe a huge thank you to retired U.S. Navy fighter pilot Vincent "Jell-O" Aiello for providing certain technical details. Also to Mark "Silky" Sileikis, PR1 U.S. Navy (retired) for his pointers about life and operations aboard a modern aircraft carrier.

Despite all this best effort, there may be technical errors, some intentional as artistic license to create a compelling, simplified story for non-aviators (such as simplification of call signs and other radio procedure), and others not intentional, with any of course being mine. If you're a military aviation buff and see any major gaffs you'd like to share, email me at Read@CraigDiLouie.com. Corrections may inform future editions of the book.

Thank you for reading!

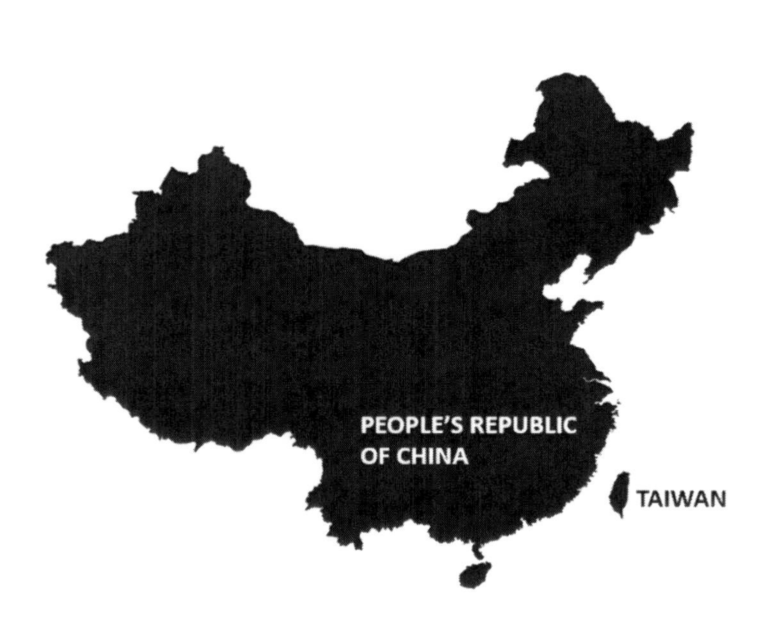
PEOPLE'S REPUBLIC
OF CHINA
TAIWAN

ONE

Let me tell you something about war, comrade: It makes a hell of a story. People will kill for a good story, and some will even die for it.

Depending on how mine turns out, I might be one of those dying.

Outside these barren walls, I am Jack Knapp, lieutenant, junior-grade, United States naval aviator. Here in the People's Republic of China, I'm Prisoner 2299, soon to be executed on trumped-up charges of crimes against humanity.

You are Deputy Bureau Chief Zhang Fang, my case officer. You serve the Ministry of State Security, one of the many departments in the leviathan that is the Chinese Communist Party (CCP).

I am at Qincheng Prison in Beijing, writing my "confession."

I live in a two hundred-square-foot cell with a toilet, bed, and an ancient typewriter set on a little writing desk. The heavy iron-plated door has peep holes and a window through which meals are served. Overhead, a single dim bulb lights the room. Two sanded glass windows, sloped to catch the sunlight, add natural illumination during the day. At the window edges, there's enough clear glass I can see the nearby mountain and sometimes the sun.

As far as living quarters go, it's not a nice place but not as bad as I'd imagined it'd be. In some ways, it's not that different than living on an aircraft carrier.

Or maybe I'm just happy the torture has stopped. Everything looks rosier when you're not getting beaten black and blue every day.

You set all this up—the typewriter, the paper, the free time to write while my trial grinds on—because you want me to tell you a story. You think if you control my story, it will help you control the story of the war. And if you control the story of the war, you can change its outcome.

I am forced to oblige, though it may not be the story you want to hear.

TWO

I'd grown up watching war movies, and then suddenly I was in one, though we weren't at war, not yet.

I was flying eight hundred feet over the Pacific at three hundred fifty knots.

Powered by nuclear reactors, the USS *Independence* steamed into the wind west of San Diego, California. Majestic and massive, the aircraft carrier loomed ten stories over the teeming sea. Seahawk helos buzzed around it.

My squadron rocketed past its starboard side, offering a view of the sprawling flight deck and the island command structure jutting from it. Crews in colorful visored helmets, jerseys, and float vests waited for us to land.

To us aviators, this massive ship was simply "the boat," which we called Mother. For nine months, this floating gray city would be my home. *Independence* and the ships in its carrier strike group were bound for the Pacific packing enough punch to level cities and cripple national economies.

The carrier had set sail with empty decks. The nine squadrons of aircraft of Carrier Air Wing Six would join her at sea.

We'd flown out from Naval Air Station Lemoore early this morning, riding high in the sky to economize on fuel. Routine flying for the senior guys, though for me the novelty hadn't yet worn off and felt like it never would.

The world, so small, had opened to reveal itself,

and I enjoyed the flight as I always did, which was like surfing the sky with the sun and the wind.

Tiger, our commander, had radioed us to pull our F/A-18 Super Hornets into formation and burn an oval in the sky until it was our turn to land. From a great altitude, the carrier had looked like a postage stamp lying on a blue-green floor.

Now we just had to land on it in one piece.

Being fresh from advanced flight training, this presented some pucker factor for me. I'd made it this far, though, and I was determined to be the best I could be, make that the best aviator in the whole—

"Try not to kill us, okay?" the WSO said from the backseat.

Pronounced *wizzo*, the WSO, or weapon systems officer, helped with observation, coordinated strikes with friendly forces during ground support missions, and performed other important jobs in the two-seat version of the Super Hornet.

My WSO for the flight was Lieutenant Jeff Wayne, call sign, "Duke."

Repeat viewings of *Top Gun* had given me the impression the WSO played the role of pilot's sidekick, my own personal wingman. More realistically, this being Duke's second sea deployment, I thought he'd be a mentor.

From the outset, he'd dispelled both notions, laughing at all my mistakes. So far, he was more like my own personal peanut gallery.

Lucky for me, he was not only my WSO but would also be one of my roommates once I'd made it aboard.

"I will certainly try," I said.

Perfect landing, I told myself over and over like

a prayer.

Tiger led us into the break in echelon-right formation. I counted seventeen seconds and then banked left. The turn completed, I leveled out flying in the opposite direction down the carrier's port side.

Ahead of me, the commander's Super Hornet appeared a black dot in the sky. I glanced at the carrier and spotted a jet taxiing along the deck, making room for the next to land. The whole thing was set up so a jet landed every sixty seconds.

I set the flaps to full to reduce my speed. I was flying only six hundred feet over the water now and wondering if I was forgetting something important.

My flight school instructor barked in my ear: *Your jet is trying to kill you! Respect it!*

On land, a pilot typically enjoys eight thousand feet of runway to arrive safely on the ground. On a thousand-foot-long carrier, we have less than three hundred.

Because of this, carriers fling jets off their decks with steam-powered catapults and snag them upon their return using hydraulic arresting cables running across the deck.

Independence used a four-wire system. The trick is to land just right so the jet's tailhook catches the wire, ideally the third one.

Put another way, it's like slamming thread at a hundred fifty miles an hour into the eye of a needle moving at around thirty.

Come in too low, you can hit the ramp and fireball. Come in just right but off the centerline, you might crash into parked aircraft.

In short, it's a challenge even for experienced aviators for whom landing is a matter of muscle memory but never routine.

So far, so good. The conditions were ideal. Clear skies with almost unlimited visibility, moderate winds and swells, the ship on a straight course…

This was doable. I'd done it before; I'd already carrier-qualified at the end of training. And my first two landings would be touch and go. I'd land, keep going, and take off again back into the pattern.

Then I'd make an arrested landing on my final run.

Doable, yes. Nonetheless, sweat poured down my face from under my oxygen mask, and my heart galloped as if trying to get onto the carrier before the rest of me did.

Guided by my resolute if sweaty hand, my jet shot past the carrier's stern and swooped into its approach turn. I'd basically circled the carrier, bleeding off airspeed and altitude before landing.

Showtime.

I worked the throttles to stay on speed while I continued to control my rate of descent with the stick between my knees.

I was approaching the groove, the final leg, everything certain of a safe landing except for maybe its green pilot.

Oh, shit.

I couldn't see the ball.

The "ball" is a system of lights mounted on the flight deck's port side that signal to pilots whether they're on the proper glide slope. The idea is to keep the amber ball centered on a row of green reference lights.

If the lights appear red, you're going too low,

which means transformation into a pink mist is imminent.

Me? I couldn't see it at all.

The LSO's voice popped onto the radio. "You're too high."

This was the landing signal officer, or LSO. Stationed on the flight deck, LSOs guide pilots during landings. They carry the nickname, "Paddles" from the old days when they used colorful paddles to provide visual guidance to pilots.

A good LSO can save your life, though he can also ruin your day. LSOs give pilots landing grades that follow them around during the deployment, make that their careers. Everybody receives them, even the veterans, as naval aviators have to constantly prove themselves worthy of their aircraft seats.

The point is that even if I didn't drill a hole in the spud locker, I could still die of shame.

I corrected with a nudge of the stick.

"Call the ball when you got it," the LSO said.

Just then, it peekabooed like a glorious sunrise, shining with amusement at the nugget howling toward it.

"Three-Oh-Seven, Rhino, ball," I rattled off, reporting my side number and aircraft type—*Rhino* being the nickname for the Super Hornet my squadron flew.

My voice sounded thin and husky from dry mouth and nerves. I might suffer death from embarrassment before I even made it aboard.

You got this, I told myself.

"Roger, ball, twenty-four knots," the LSO replied, informing me of the wind speed over the flight deck.

Otherwise, he sounded dubious that I did in fact have it.

The carrier's stern grew larger by the second as I corrected and then corrected again after I overcorrected. Boeing designed the Super Hornet with a digital fly-by-wire system, in which even a small movement of the stick has dramatic repercussions in how the jet responds.

The closer you get to the carrier, the smaller the corrections you're supposed to make.

I could feel my dwindling margin of error breathing down my neck.

"You're high," the LSO corrected me. "*Easy*... Come left ... back to the right ... back to the left, *easy* corrections... You're on..."

Ahead, the expanding steel slab, awash in late summer sunshine, gleamed in morning gold. My bulging eyes took in the painted foul lines on the angled deck, the wires strung across the runway, the jets parked with their wings folded up.

Then I shut it all out, keeping my eyes glued to the *ball, ball, ball*—

My hand twitching with tiny corrections to stay zeroed while blood and adrenaline and terror roared in my ears—

Cowabunga!

THUMP!

The tires slammed the deck.

Touchdown.

I gasped in stunned disbelief. The training took over, and I pushed the throttles to full power and closed the flaps. My burner cans flared behind me as my Rhino roared down the runway and left the bow.

Then I breathed again, wings level and climbing back to six hundred feet.

The second touch and go went better. When it came time to do it for real and catch the arresting wire, I was loaded for bear.

Ahead of the approach turn, I dropped the tailhook and landing gear and reset the flaps to full.

Then I was back in the groove, riding the ball all the way to touchdown.

My wheels slammed the deck the final time. I throttled to full power, this time in case I had to get back in the air because of an emergency, trusting the wire to stop me from doing it.

The burner cans roared as my Rhino jerked to a sudden lurching halt, like a charging horse responding to a sudden pull of the reins. My body strained against the belts as my sixteen-ton jet went from a hundred fifty to zero miles per hour in two seconds.

I'd done it. I'd made the trap.

The blessed tailhook had caught the lovely third wire.

After throttling back, I raised my fist and whooped.

Duke cleared his throat, a subtle reminder that maybe I should celebrate later. Another plane would be coming in right behind me in less than a minute, and I had to get out of the way.

A yellow shirt signaled me with growing impatience. These guys were the traffic cops of the flight deck.

Stupidly, I replied with a salute. I felt light as a breeze. *What's that, my good man? You want me to taxi where directed? Of course, of course.*

I unlocked and folded the wings and rolled to my

parking space, where I held the brake until the crew secured the plane with blocks and chains. Then I whooped again while Duke sighed.

Right now, I was a god.

Opening the canopy, I hauled my sweat-soaked body out of the cockpit. The air reeked of jet fuel and exhaust and my personal funk, which practically steamed off me as I descended the boarding ladder.

My WSO plopped down next to me. "Not bad for a nugget. Come on, let's go debrief—"

"Hang on." I jogged to the front of the plane and fist bumped the nose like a dork.

Now, I'd heard some aviators did this as an intimate good luck or thank-you ritual, and if they did I was sure they made it look cool, but I wasn't cool, not yet. But for that single moment on the chaotic flight deck, tingling from head to toe, I was the star of this movie, intensely alive and filled with awareness of destiny.

Duke didn't wait. He was already walking away. The next Super Hornet whumped down onto the deck and lurched to a halt on the arresting wire.

I ran to catch up. "Do you think I'll get an OK from Paddles?" An okay was the best landing grade one could hope for.

"Maybe," the WSO said.

"Any advice for me?"

Duke stopped to stare at me. "You have to find your own way, Knapp."

"Come on, man. I just need a little help navigating all this."

He sighed again. "All right. I remember what it was like on my first deployment. I'll help you out, but don't tell anybody I did."

"I swear."

"Don't worry about Paddles, worry about the skipper." The skipper was our commanding officer, or CO. "If you want to butter him up, be upfront with self-criticism. Show him you aren't a diva. Then he can better help you level up."

"Thanks, Duke!"

"Don't mention it. And I mean, don't."

It was great advice.

God, was I ever dumb for ever trusting Duke.

THREE

In battle, you're willing to kill and die for the guy next to you, but that doesn't necessarily mean you like him very much.

After the last landing, Duke and I squeezed into the crowded paraloft to stow our G-suits and harnesses, and then made our way into our ready room.

Independence housed nine such rooms, one for each squadron, including my VFA-95, the "Gargoyles," scourge of dictators, terror of the Pacific, envy of the Fleet, avatars of Mars, beloved by women and poets, etc., etc.

These officers manned and supported operations for a dozen F/A-18 Super Hornets.

The ready room functioned as meeting space and lounge. Though I'd seen it before, my shining nugget eyes took it all in again with a sense of wonder.

It was a typical compartment in an aircraft carrier, which is to say utilitarian, ugly, and battleship gray, with LED lights and acoustical panels hanging below gurgling pipes and ventilation ducts running along the overhead.

The vents blasted air conditioning, one of the luxuries of living on a nuclear-powered carrier, though depending on where you went on the big boat, this usually meant either roasting or freezing. Rows of chairs faced front, where briefings or instruction occurred using a projection screen. Behind the chairs stood the duty desk, a foosball table, coffee, and a computer you could use to check out the internet if you didn't mind the horrendously slow speed.

I ignored most of this, focusing instead on the trophies and awards and photos. There was history in this room, and history to be made.

The squadron's insignia, a nasty little winged red monster on a black field, dominated one wall along with a series of mounted plaques and unit decorations. Under them, a glass case mysteriously displayed a series of wrenches. A board presented the day's flight schedule written out in grease pencil.

The TV was currently set to play the live feed from cameras on the flight deck, showing a Super Hornet hitting the roof with a boom that vibrated down the ready room's bulkheads.

And then there was the greenie board, which displayed the LSO landing grades for each pilot in the squadron. Green was good, yellow fair, red bad, and brown a "turd."

This was the clubhouse, and I was now a member. I am not embarrassed to say I was a little drunk at that moment, my face feverish with pride.

A Gargoyle elbowed me out of his way. "Make a hole."

I'd been blocking the entrance like a tourist. Sobering up a little, I stowed my helmet and nav bag.

My helmet had KNAPP stenciled on the back, the proud label of a long lineage of losers from York, Maryland that had produced me. My call sign in flight school was Hoser, the result of my fuel hose refusing to retract after an air refueling and me landing with it swinging wildly around my aircraft's nose.

Here, I didn't have a call sign, as I wasn't a person yet. To the Navy, I was a nugget, meaning a newbie on his first deployment, a diamond in the rough awaiting a polish.

To these Gargoyles, however, I was FNG. A Fucking New Guy.

I considered this a challenge. I was going to prove myself. I'd signed up for the Navy to do just this, but over time, I'd started to confuse proving something to me with proving it to everybody else.

I didn't know it at the time, but I wanted a sense of human belonging and basic peer approval way more than I wanted to be a sky god. What I also didn't know was the harder you tried to fit in, the less you did.

Hindsight is clarifying and oh so humbling.

Still, wanting to prove myself one way or the other at the time wasn't a bad thing. The Navy didn't go in for the *Top Gun* crap, it wanted its aviators to work together as a team, but everybody wanted to be the best. There was a whole lot of competition here and a definite pecking order, in which I was starting at the bottom near the bilge.

I could practically smell the competition along with all the sweat and testosterone. Pilots are often Type A overachiever types, each of them God's gift to the world of military aviation, and their approval had to be earned.

The skipper chatted with the pilots while the LSO doled out their landing grades and Johnny Cash's "The Man Comes Around" played over the room's sound system to mark the occasion.

While many aviators have a call sign with some embarrassing story attached, our CO seemingly didn't, as *Tiger* is what we call an aggressive pilot. He appeared built from muscle and rope and exuded a barely bridled fury. The skipper wore the circular black-and-red TOPGUN patch, which marked him as a graduate of the Navy's elite fighter weapons school.

It was like looking at the *Top Gun* movies' Maverick himself, though without the arrogance and lack of regard for basic flight safety. He didn't know it yet, but Tiger was destined to be my *sensei*, my bildungsroman father figure. I was already prepared to kill for a single "attaboy" from him.

Next to him, the dapper executive officer (XO), sporting a wispy deployment mustache, stood with his arms crossed, chiming in to amplify or try to soften what the skipper said. Behind their backs, we called them *Mom and Dad.*

Another one of my bunkmates and a buddy from my replacement squadron, fellow nugget Lieutenant, junior-grade Jordan Morrison approached me looking glum. "I got a fair pass, amigo." Yellow on the board.

"Fair is good enough," I said and quoted the general rule, "Any landing you walk away from is a good landing."

"Yeah." He really was down about it. The eldest son in a Navy family, he had a lot to live up to.

"Seriously, you made the trap. Be proud of that."

"How'd you do?"

"Don't know yet. I was on autopilot and crapping myself during most of it."

I decided to take my own advice to be happy I'd made the trap and survived.

"I'm sure you did all right," Morrison said, showing he could bullshit as well as I could.

The Gargoyles bled away after getting their grades until it was my turn. I faced the LSO, ready to have a candid conversation about my performance as a pilot, even if it meant taking criticism.

"Three-Oh-Seven." Wearing a white jersey, the LSO flipped through a little black notebook, on which my grade was written in shorthand. "High start, too much power on come down in the middle. Overall, I'd call it a nice pass."

I'd earned a green button with a "4" on it, which would be placed on the greenie board. I accepted this news like he was promoting me. "Thank you."

The LSO eyed me. "Any parting shots?"

This was my chance to give feedback as Duke had advised, and I could get some work done in the self-improvement department. I offered an admittedly longwinded explanation for the high start, swore to improve, and asked if he had any pointers that would help me develop as an aviator.

The LSO blinked before turning to Tiger with an incredulous smile. Tiger stared at me, a little dimple winking on his chiseled jaw. He was grinding his big molars, and I was starting to wonder if I'd said something wrong. Next to the skipper, the XO stood smiling with his arms crossed.

"Just keep it up." The LSO chuckled as he stood to exit. This was not his circus, and I was not his monkey.

"I have some feedback for you, Knapp," the skipper growled. "You ready for it?"

I leaned forward and put on my most earnest expression. "Yes, sir."

He snapped his fingers.

I blinked. "Sir?"

He snapped his fingers again. "There's your feedback."

I thought I understood. *Just do the job*, he was saying. *Don't overthink it.* It was good feedback. "Thank you, Skipper."

The executive officer cackled and then cut it off to scowl at Duke sitting behind me. "As for you, you're on my shit list."

Duke replied with his best insolent smirk. "Is there a problem, XO?"

"I'm looking around this ready room, but I don't see the skipper's TOPGUN trophy on the wall. You were supposed to get it out of storage."

"I, uh, just boarded, XO."

"It was supposed to be on display *before* the Boat embarked."

"And I've got a full duty—"

"Well, somebody has to get it. This is about the squadron's honor."

"I'll get it, XO," I chimed in.

"Outstanding, Knapp." The XO punctuated this with a curt nod of approval. "Consider it an opportunity to excel."

"Where will I find it?"

"It's in compartment PL." He swiveled his gaze back to Duke. "You stick around. We want to talk to you."

"I'm all yours," the WSO said.

I watched all this, unsure what to do next.

"You'd better get a move on, Knapp," the XO told me. "The next time I see you, there should be a trophy in your mitts all shiny and in one piece, okay?"

"Sir!" I jumped out of my chair.

Thus began a strange journey through the maze.

An aircraft carrier is a *big* place.

Home to around six thousand crew and airmen, *Independence* was eleven hundred feet long, with a two hundred fifty-foot width that tapered to about half that at the waterline. Endless passageways wormed through its steel guts, labeled with bullseye orientation codes—if there was one thing the Navy had more of than bombs and bullets, it was codes, call signs, acronyms, and bullshit—all taking you to innumerable compartments, like some kind of giant floating anthill.

What had I gotten myself into?

I had no idea where compartment PL was, and asking mom and dad for directions was out of the question.

It may seem I'd volunteered to score points, but mostly I just wanted to see the skipper's TOPGUN trophy. I could imagine it from repeat viewings of the *Top Gun* movie, where the best aviator in his class won the honor.

A metal fighter jet mounted on a wood plaque with the words, TOPGUN, UNITED STATES NAVY WEAPONS SCHOOL, and then the winner's name.

I know it sounds stupid, but I wanted to touch it in the hopes its luck would rub off on me. I've always been a little superstitious when it comes to flying.

I was on the Mess Deck level, which housed the air wing's ready rooms, staterooms, and squadron stores along with command areas. Aircraft landed with heavy thuds on the flight deck above. I figured the trophy couldn't be far from the ready room, so I decided to wander around until I bumped into PL.

The ship's crew was out in full force, crowding the narrow, industrial passageways like a social experiment in courtesy or maybe a low-budget dystopia. Every so often, the passageway cut through a ship frame complete with a thick watertight door and oval-shaped hatch opening you had to step through, hopefully without knocking your knees.

I knocked them anyway, gathering bruises as I crossed the deck.

As Navy courtesy required enlisted personnel make way for officers except in an emergency, I drilled a hole for most of my journey, but since I didn't know where I wanted to go, I only made things even more awkward. The ship had its own rhythm, and I was still learning its tempo.

The tiling soon turned from gray to blue, indicating I'd walked all the way to the command areas. I snagged a pair of sailors. "Hey, guys, I'm looking for PL."

The younger of the two had no idea where it was, but the seadog did. "You got a ways to go, sir. That compartment is on the second deck."

I groaned. This was going to take forever. I headed to the nearest ladderwell and plowed four levels down using steep stairs that were actually tilted ladders, which promised to make my return trip feel like mountain climbing.

On Deck Two was another officers' wardroom, more staterooms, and the berthing where the hardworking sailors of *Independence* slept stacked like sardines and lived like mole people, as most of them wouldn't see the sun for months and survived on vitamin D supplements. In a mess room, chief petty officers chowed down cafeteria style, reminding me I was missing lunch.

The next sailor I asked about PL told me it was on

the third deck.

I fumed at this crap news. "Seriously?"

The sailor shrugged and even looked amused. "It's a big ship, sir."

"No kidding." I was exhausted now from the long walk and endless plunges through the frames.

Nothing to do for it except carry on.

Deck Three was warmer than the rest of the Boat. While landing aircraft sounded as distant, muffled thumps here, it was loud with the hum of colossal machines. The humid air smelled like oil, sweat, paint, and metal.

These were the departments that kept the ship floating and fighting. Mechanical, electrical, air-conditioning, it was all here, along with a post office, medical and dental facilities, ship's laundry, and a bank of satellite phones to call home.

Failing to see PL stenciled anywhere on the bullseyes, I snagged a machinist and asked directions. I hoped she wouldn't send me down to Deck Four, which housed the nuke reactors and ammunition magazines, or worse, back to Deck One.

"Yes, sir," the woman drawled, all sunshine. "First right after the junction."

Thank God. I was drenched in sweat again. Hurrying past her, I entered the compartment to find a burly sailor in dark blue overalls sitting at a workstation, painstakingly pecking keys on his computer by the light of a task lamp.

He squinted at me over gleaming reading glasses. "Can I help you, sir?"

I cast my bleak gaze across the cramped compartment. No joy. Nothing but tools, filing, and a few workstations. "Yeah. I'm looking for my skipper's TOPGUN trophy. VFA-95. Is this PL?"

The man grinned. "You found it."

"What is this place? What does PL stand for?"

"Oh, it's the plumbing department, sir."

Then it hit me.

In aviator lingo, a "plumber" is an inept pilot.

The whole thing had been a snipe hunt.

A joke on the nugget.

"Oh, shit." There was nothing else to say. I'd volunteered for this.

The sailor chuckled. "Don't sweat it. The XO gets somebody almost every year, zeroes in on some eager beaver. It's sort of tradition with your squadron. It's been going on so long, half the ship's crew is in on it."

"It's a good joke. Real funny." I wanted to die.

"You understand there is no TOPGUN trophy, right? It was just in the movie."

"Of course!" I mean, I certainly did now. "Thanks for your time."

"Hang on," the sailor told me. It wasn't over yet. He rooted around in a toolbox and handed me a wrench. "Your XO expects you to bring this back with you."

I realized that even after everything I'd accomplished, I was an Academy plebe again. I trudged back to the ladderwell to make the return journey.

Along the way, I grumbled imaginary speeches about how morale should be inspired and not taken for granted, and how I was here to learn and fight for my country, not get sent on wild goose chases for a cheap laugh.

All of which, if actually spoken, would only make me look even more stupid.

Another appealing option was to dive overboard and swim back to San Diego, but that was another no-go.

Which really left only one option. Suck it up.

In fact, I'd show them I was a good sport. The only acceptable response you can give to this type of programmed humiliation is to laugh along with it.

So that's what I did.

When I walked into the ready room, the sight of my sheepish smile sent the squadron roaring to its feet. I held the wrench over my head as if the TOPGUN trophy existed and I'd won it, while the Gargoyles pelted me with crumpled-up pieces of paper, a mock ritual stoning that ended with good-natured laughter and a few soda cans raised in a toast.

Duke gave me one. "Welcome to the Gargoyles."

I drank and belched into my hand. "Yeah, I'm feeling the love."

The XO strolled over. "You got something for me, Knapp?"

I handed him the wrench. "I didn't have time to shine it, sir."

He chuckled and patted my shoulder before walking away to add it to the other wrenches in the squadron's display case. Standing on the far side of the room, even Tiger looked amused.

"They got me too, my first deployment," Duke assured me. "Don't sweat it."

"I won't." I had been, but honestly I wasn't anymore. By being the butt of the joke, I'd discovered a strange kind of acceptance. "You were an eager beaver?" Honestly, it was hard to picture him that way.

"Nope. The XO doesn't just get the beavers." The

WSO grinned. "He gets whoever he thinks needs to learn a lesson in humility."

Maybe I wasn't humble enough? I flashed back to the debrief. "What was the skipper trying to tell me when he snapped his fingers?"

He guffawed. "Ah. Yeah. SNAP."

"Right, he snapped his fingers—"

"No. SNAP. S-N-A-P. Sensitive New Age Pilot."

The Navy loved its acronyms.

It turned out that aside from essential communication, the skipper didn't want to hear my perceptions and feelings and requests for feedback at all, and now regarded me as a weak sister.

FOUR

Battles aren't always fought in wars. Sometimes, you find yourself fighting one right at home, against people on your own side.

Independence went to sea, and I was going with her.

For the next nine months, like a cop on his beat, we'd cruise around the Pacific Ocean to ensure freedom of navigation and regional adherence to international law.

We'd snuggle Hawaii and Guam, wave at Japan, comfort Taiwan, glare at North Korea, conduct joint exercises with the Republic of Korea Navy, and drop anchor at Busan for some liberty and a little tourism.

As for me, I was finally in the game. Carrier-qualified and feeling my oats, I reported to my squadron ready room. The day's flight schedule had me paired up with Duke for a sortie. I'd be taking part in the combat air patrol, or CAP, that kept the carrier safe.

I checked in with the duty officer and received a Beretta and magazines from the gun safe, which I'd carry on the flight.

My WSO sat in his big leather chair, watching the pilots' landing aid television (PLAT) screen with some other guys, who commented on the topside landings like sports commentators.

Fed by cameras on the flight deck, the PLAT is like the channel in the hotel that's about the hotel, only far more popularly watched, particularly during bad conditions that made for varsity landings.

I checked the screen myself to update on the weather. Another sunny day in the Pacific, ideal for flying.

Duke crammed a handful of potato chips into his mouth and munched, his eyes glued to the screen. "Ready to fly the friendly skies?"

"I'm spring loaded," I said, a bit too earnestly.

WHAM!

On the PLAT, a Super Hornet had struck the roof and fired its burner cans until yanked to a stop by the arresting wire. The bang vibrated down the ready room bulkheads.

Nobody even blinked at the noise, though if any civilians were here, they'd swear a bomb had blown the ship's stern off.

"Wait until you see how she flies today," Duke said. "You'll thank me."

The WSO had advised me to request a tune-up of my jet. *Just tell Riggs something doesn't feel right*, he'd told me after our last flight together.

That way, he added, I'd be ahead of the curve when other jets started to break down during the deployment.

We don't always use the same jet—in fact, we often fly whatever's handy and prepped for us to use—so I wasn't sure his advice would give me a real edge.

It had a certain logic, though, and if it's one thing Duke seemed to know something about, it was how to work the system. So on impulse, I went for it.

Aviation Machinist's Mate Airman Sam Riggs was my plane captain, a tall, lanky teenager wearing a brown jersey and visored helmet. His youth hadn't surprised me; the average age on the flight deck was around nineteen.

He was clearly puzzled by my request, and I wondered if I'd stepped in it, but I was committed, so I kept at it. It went on like that until Bryant, the bearish maintenance master chief, showed up, crossed his arms over his ample gut, and ordered Sam to comply, as I was an officer and lawful orders were orders and he'd better hop to it because that's how the Navy worked.

In the end, I felt guilty about the whole thing, but today I might be piloting a fully tuned-up jet that would keep me alive and allow me to fly my best.

The aviators roared at the PLAT. On the screen, the next jet had missed the wire and boltered, its tailhook scraping the deck in a faint trail of sparks.

"Ouch," Duke said. "Who is that?"

"Dunno," Dangle answered. "He's with the Marine squadron riding with us."

"Screw him, then."

The men chuckled. I glanced at the greenie board, where my name had a line of green buttons next to it.

I now had a goal.

While I'd finally made it to the show, I was still a junior officer, or JO; a wingman; a nugget. A few of the senior aviators I inevitably annoyed sometimes called me "FNG," though my individuality was now recognized with the label "FNG4," as there were three other such Fucking New Guys on the Boat, all of us interchangeable and best seen doing our jobs and not heard.

That's not to say I didn't have intimate, bonding conversations about tactics and procedures and whatnot with these guys, but they usually went like this: *FNG4 is impressing exactly zero personnel. FNG4 should shut up and learn. FNG4 should answer the phone, and if the duty officer wants to task a JO, he should suck it up and consider said tasking an opportunity to excel.*

The only way to fast-track my acceptance was to do just that. Excel.

In the air, I was a typical nugget. I sometimes lost my flight lead in the clouds and had to find him, which is harder than it sounds. Once—again in the clouds—I drifted too close to my lead, which earned me another ass-chewing. And it took me too long to do the high-speed midair surgery that was in-flight refueling from an aerial tanker.

On my landings, though, I was a goddamn wizard so far. I even squeaked out OKs on my night landings, including one without the benefit of moonlight, which is terrifying because it's blacker than smoke blown up the skipper's ass and you're flying on instruments alone.

The pilots disparaged the greenie board as the product of opinion but kept keen tabs anyway. Despite teamwork being necessary to mission success and personal survival, competition was king. Pilots were judged on everything and under constant pressure to perform.

My dream was to earn a place in the Air Wing Top Ten for landings, rocketing from nugget to a pack leader. Unlikely if not impossible, but once the idea popped into my head, I couldn't let go of it. By the grace of God, I'd go even further, maybe even reaching for the number one spot, the Top Hook—

Pop, operations officer, section leader, and my flight lead on today's patrol, interrupted this fantasy in his Texan drawl. "You're holding us up, Knapp."

"Yes, sir! Come on, Duke."

"Yup." The WSO's cheeks bulged with a final loading of potato chips.

Pepsi Man showed up, followed by Siren, his WSO, who'd earned her *nom de guerre* on account of her throaty, distractingly sexy voice on the radio.

Dressed in our green flight suits and holding our nav bags, the five of us made our way to the paraloft to wrestle into our gear.

Today, Pop would fly his single-seater, me and Duke our two-seater. Our jets constituted the patrol; Pepsi Man and Siren would catapult after us as a spare in case either jet had any trouble.

By the time I was ready, I wore fifty pounds of gear: helmet, flight suit and gloves, G suit around my legs and waist to prevent blacking out while pulling high Gs, ejection harness, survival vest, life preserver, oxygen mask, brown aviator boots, and Garmin watch that not only told the time but measured air pressure.

Meanwhile, in my bag, I'd brought charts, manuals, piddle pack should I have to whizz during the long flight, snacks, and a brown-bag lunch.

We mounted the ladder and stepped onto the flight deck. My Spidey sense tingled as I took in a multitude of threats. In one sense, an aircraft carrier is a platform for launching and recovering aircraft. In another, it's a violent industrial world that batters and occasionally tries to kill you.

On a carrier, accidents happen every day, crushed fingers and toes for the most part, sometimes the odd daydreaming sailor who walks into a missile fin and gashes his nose, but other times, a misstep can get you killed.

Getting run over by a taxiing jet, torched by flaming burner cans, sucked into a jet's turbine intake, slashed by an E-2's spinning props, or falling off the edge of the world were all possibilities guaranteed to ruin somebody's day.

Navigating these hazards, Duke and I reached our plane. My heart swelled with happiness when I beheld JACK KNAPP stenciled on the side. I couldn't wait to get in the cockpit and fly it.

A brown shirt welcomed me with a jaunty salute and offered her hand, which I shook. Holly Young.

"Good morning, sir," she said sunnily. "How are you today?"

"I'm great! How are—"

"Your load is fourteen-four, your battery is good, and the wing fold switch is in the folded position." I could see for myself that the wings were indeed folded, which was customary on the flight deck as it allowed more aircraft to park in the limited amount of space available.

"Perfect!" I said.

I pivoted into my preflight inspection. Duke and I were about to kick the tires and light the fires, as the saying went, and this was the program's tire-kicking portion.

We circled the plane, running our hands over everything to make sure there were no missing fasteners or stress cracks or any other problems, and generally confirming that we could trust this machine with our lives.

Not that we needed to today. This baby had been given a thorough going-over by the grease monkeys.

Satisfied, we mounted the boarding ladders and dropped into our cockpits. Jammed in with charts and bags wedged against me, I felt more like baggage than pilot, at least while I was on the deck. I plugged in my oxygen hose, a life-saving device as the air starts to get mighty thin above ten thousand feet.

Sam mounted the ladder to help me buckle up. "It's a good day to fly, sir."

I was practically boiling with excitement. "I'm a lucky man."

He tugged to make sure I was secured, a gesture that reminded me of a dad tucking in his unruly kid. "You're good to go."

"Hey, thanks for giving the bird a good going-over. I really appreciate it."

"It's all part of the job, sir." Then he gave the jet a loving pat and was gone.

I admired Sam for being a good sport. More than a hundred fifty sailors kept the squadron in the air, and among the most important were the plane captains, modern-day squires in service to knights who rode the winds.

I literally couldn't do this without him and all the other support personnel inspecting my plane, checking its fluid levels, keeping the flight deck clear of debris that could get sucked into engine, and preparing the cockpit for flight.

In short, I owed him a big one, the first among many I knew I'd end up owing him.

Closing the canopy, I strapped on my thigh boards and conducted preflight instrument checks. Behind me, Duke checked and rechecked our systems.

"START TO GO AIRCRAFT," the Air Boss said over the 5MC loudspeaker from his control center perched atop the island. "START THEM UP."

I waggled three fingers to signal Sam I was starting the auxiliary power unit, or APU. Once the APU green light blinked on, I waggled two fingers to start engine two and then just my index finger for engine one.

Both engines responded with an aerosol hum, and I could feel their power flowing through the airframe and into my racing heart. In my cockpit, Bitching Betty, the auto voice warning system, welcomed me in an arresting Tennessee twang: *Flight controls. Flight controls.*

It made me a little homesick; she sounded exactly like my mom, who'd grown up in a little town outside Nashville.

The hydraulic systems checked out, and we started flight control sequencing. Sam circled the jet, eyeing the nooks and crannies for problems that could ruin your day at twenty thousand feet. Grinning like an idiot, I waited to be told to taxi to the catapult.

I was finally in the real show. A lot of hard work had led up to this.

Ever since I was a kid and saw the Blue Angels fly at the Flying Circus airshow, I'd wanted to be a pilot. I'd grown up in a small town steamrolled by recession: shuttered businesses, crumbling houses, a potholed main drag, all of it awash in American flags.

After high school, I didn't have money for college, and local job prospects sucked. I'd gotten good grades at school but had nowhere to go. The military offered a path, which is how I ended up becoming the sorry property of the Navy.

I went to the Academy full of excitement—it's no easy thing to get in, so I felt like I'd won the lottery.

My plebe summer squeezed out and stomped on any such joy. After weeks of hazing by cadres screaming at me for everything from a piece of lint on my uniform to wearing a shit-eating grin, I understood the whole thing was specially designed not to develop my potential but flush me out. They weren't molding me, they were telling me to mold or get the hell off their lawn.

I hated it. I don't know why I stuck with it. I guess I didn't have anything else. Back home, all my high school friends were doing a little this, a little that, and generally getting high whenever they could. Their aimless wandering to a dead end started to sound mighty appealing, but I wasn't willing to surrender my childish dream of surfing the roof of the world.

I suffered through it.

I learned how to wax a floor to a blinding gleam and make a bed you could bounce a quarter from and about a hundred different varied and wondrous ways to eat shit—from basic drive-through shit all the way to gourmet, five-course shit with a fragrant shit dessert. I discovered how many push-ups I could do before I was smoked, and that even when the cadres joked it was best to stay grim and never laugh.

By the end of plebe summer, our band of forty desperate and strung-out kids dwindled to thirty-two.

During my years at the Academy as a midshipman, I learned how to string sentences together and read literature as part of my English degree. After graduation, I finally got where I wanted to go, which was flight school. From plebe to midshipman to ensign, I was moving up in the world.

First stop was preflight indoctrination in Pensacola, followed by two years at various flight schools and training bases in Texas. Aviators list their preference for aircraft assignment; for me, it was always jets.

I exceled in advanced flight training. Only a small fraction of people who want to fly jets get to do it, and I worked my ass off to stand among the lucky few. My head buzzed with aerodynamics, weather, navigation, and flight regulations.

I graduated as a lieutenant, junior-grade. I'd earned my wings, so to speak but also literally, gold wings I wore with pride. Even so, still my preparation for the real world wasn't over, as I had to put in another six months in a fleet replacement squadron and train on the ferocious, fanged beast that was the F/A-18 Super Hornet before being assigned to VFA-95.

After completing enough schooling I could have become a lawyer instead, I felt like I was grown up and ready to play the game of war.

Imagine that for seven years you're the understudy for a leading role in Broadway's hottest play, and then you finally saunter onto the stage to deliver your lines. That's the only way I can think of to describe how awesome I felt sitting on the flight deck with my jet warmed up, ready to launch into the big blue for my first CAP.

"Hey," Duke said in the backseat. "What's he doing here?"

Maintenance Master Chief Bryant strolled into the area and whistled at Sam, who hustled over. The plane captain's helmeted head bobbed as he listened.

Then he turned and raised his hands with his wrists crossed. He was suspending the launch. I shut down the engines and APU.

"What's going on?" I called to Sam.

He jerked his thumb like an umpire. *You're out.* "Hydraulic leak, sir! We can't launch your bird."

What the hell? I flushed with rage. *Hydraulic leak?* They'd just given the jet a good going-over! Pepsi Man and Siren would now take my place on the flight while I watched them do it on the PLAT in the ready room.

Then I looked over and caught the evil grin on Bryant's wide face.

If you want to learn a lesson, join the Navy. It has tons of teachers.

I was learning one right now.

"The plane is down," Duke said cheerfully in the rear cockpit. "How about that? It appears we have the day off."

He always knew how to work the system.

I turned my head as far as it would go. "Hey, Duke?"

"Yeah?"

"Fuck you, man."

He chuckled. "You *did* ask me to help you learn the ropes, nugget."

FIVE

A particularly hard truth I've learned about conflict is that sometimes, you lose. The trick isn't how to avoid losing, as you can't, but how to do it with grace.

Thanks to Duke's trickery and my foolishness, I found myself grounded for the day, which led to me meeting the Valkyries.

With nothing to do, I put on service khakis and volunteered as the squadron duty officer behind a desk in the ready room, overseeing the day's flight operations. I wrote down flight hours in the book and handed out guns and ammo from the safe.

When I had a few spare moments, I bored holes in the back of Duke's chair with my evil glare.

As duty officer, I acted with the commander's authority, and I prayed for a juicy bullshit tasking to come down the pipe for which I'd need somebody to "volunteer."

As Duke was presently unoccupied, he made a natural choice. I'd stick the tasking straight up his ass.

Humiliation is bitter, but revenge is sweet and cold as ice cream.

As if sensing I had him in radar lock, the WSO took a break from the PLAT and twisted in his chair to gaze blandly into my wicked smile. "Hey, Knapp."

"What?"

"You want some advice?"

My wicked smile turned into a murderous grin.

A handful of popcorn disappeared into his fat yap. "Tell Pop the maintenance chief screwed you." As operations officer, Pop was in charge of the flight schedule. "The skipper can't have his pilots grounded."

Yelling an obscenity would draw too much attention from the other aviators hanging around the clubhouse, so I did the next best thing and flipped him the bird to express as best I was able my expert opinion on him advising me anymore.

He chuckled. "Bryant holds grudges. Who knows how long you'll end up with jet problems? Better get used to flying that desk. In fact, you should sign up for as much duty officer time as you can get. You know, to be useful."

The more time I spent as squadron duty officer, the less he and the other aviators would have to do it. More advice I didn't need.

"You'll be the one volunteering as soon as I get a good tasking," I gloated. I was blowing the surprise, but I couldn't help myself.

"You won't be tasking *me*, man. Check the board. I'm going up with Sparky after your shift."

Sputtering, I wheeled to take in the day's flight schedule. Sure enough, there was the WSO's name in blocky capitals written with grease pencil. "How?"

His shoulders lilted in a lazy shrug.

Duke always knew how to work the system.

"You want to hear *my* advice?" I snarled.

"Really nice weather for flying today," he said, gazing wistfully off into the distance as if picturing zooming across the sky. "I can't wait to get out there."

Turning purple with helpless rage, I weighed a multitude of acidic comebacks, each more lame than the next. Truth be told, I had nothing.

The WSO had already turned back to the PLAT.

He didn't care. None of it was personal for him. He just liked screwing with people to entertain himself when he was bored, which was most of the time. And he'd only screwed with me because I'd let him.

Soon after that, I was relieved, and I didn't care to hang around and watch Duke strut out to glory in his flight suit. I returned to my stateroom to find Morrison sitting cross-legged on his rack, eyes closed while he gesticulated.

"What are you doing?" I said.

"Chair flying, amigo." He clenched his eyes tighter and mumbled to himself.

This is a technique pilots used to stay mentally limber and build muscle memory. They imagine themselves in the cockpit and walking through all the myriad, mind-numbing procedures involved from takeoff to landing.

"Shoot down Kim Jong-un for me," I said.

My own chair flying often involved a detour into a dogfighting fantasy against North Korean MiG-29 pilots. At this stage of the deployment, most of our classroom briefs were about that particular dystopia and its history, military capabilities, and current threat level.

"Right now, I'm chair *landing*." Poor Morrison's landing grades remained on the weaker side. In his mind, he landed again and again, racking up a perfect record that he hoped would translate into reality.

I climbed onto my bunk, which was above his, and stretched out to stare at the piping and conduit that snaked along the overhead.

Welcome to a JO's stateroom, where six young men live in three hundred fifty square feet of depressing, drab metal dormitory. Picture stacked bunks, sinks, bulkheads plastered in fraying motivational (risqué) posters, a questionable coffee maker, dumbbells, computers on tiny desks, and an intra-ship phone.

Being under the runway track of one of the steam-powered catapults, the room was always sweltering despite the air conditioning, and it smelled about how you'd expect, like socks that ran a marathon in a sweaty jockstrap.

When you're grounded, this place feels more like a floating prison than a warship. As big as it is, a carrier is a small world. And as crowded as it is, I was dying of loneliness.

Overhead, the catapult shuttle clacked as it retracted. The green shirts were up there getting set to launch another plane. I wondered if it was Sparky and Duke, making their final checks before vaulting into open sky.

"It's not fair," I whined. While Morrison visualized his landing, I pictured Master Chief Bryant's big buzzcut head with his wide smile as smug as the Cheshire Cat's while it decapitated the Dormouse for sport. Putting the *petty* in chief petty officer. Everybody's story has a villain, and he and Duke were in the running for mine. "The maintenance guys are supposed to keep the Boat combat-effective. He's hurting himself as much as me."

"Three-Oh-Five, Rhino, ball, five-point-two," Morrison murmured.

"You know what the Navy spent on four years at the Academy and all the rest for me? Two million bucks. Plus a cool eighty million for the jet. All of it going to waste because I hurt a grown man's precious feelings."

"Damn it," Morrison said. "I just vaporized in a ramp strike."

"I just don't get it. I'm stuck here, man."

"I did it on purpose so I wouldn't have to hear you bitch anymore."

Still flushed and sweaty from a long flight, Pepsi Man, another roommate in my crowded stateroom, strolled in. "Look at these sorry specimens. The Navy keeps lowering its standards."

"Leave me alone," Morrison said, as if this were possible on an aircraft carrier.

Overhead, the jet raced down the catapult track and took to the air with a roar.

"Be the ball, that's my advice." Pepsi Man plopped in front of one of the desks to check his email. While it took forever downloading, he turned to gaze my way. "Couldn't get it up today, huh?"

"I was red-tagged on account of gremlins."

The pilot chuckled as he clacked keys on the laptop.

"Hahaha!" I said. "The newbie's suffering is so hilarious."

I should have expected no less. As the old joke went, if you want sympathy in the Navy, you can find it in the dictionary between *shit* and *syphilis*.

"What FNG4 *should* do is suck it up and use his time wisely in a similar composition as per what FNG2 here is currently conducting in his *mind*."

"Trying to," Morrison grumbled.

"I'm not in the mood, Pepsi, unless you have something constructive to say," I said.

"FNG4 should understand that is *exactly* what the more senior pilot is offering," he pontificated. "What the senior pilot is *saying* is our crap carpet is dirty, and this poses a detriment to *combat-readiness*. The senior pilot is advising FNG4 that he should procure a *vacuum cleaner for the room*."

Screw Bryant and Duke and screw him too. I set my jaw and fixed the big pipe over my bunk with a stubborn glare.

"FNG4 should consider himself *tasked*," said Pepsi Man.

"Fine!" I exploded, my shout ringing off the bulkheads.

I jumped down from my rack in a homicidal rage that had no target. We may have been pigs, but constant cleaning is a part of life on a Navy ship. What is swept can be wiped, and what is wiped can be polished to a blinding gleam.

Morrison and I were the new guys, so guess who had to do a lot of the cleaning.

I stomped outside to grab this fresh opportunity to excel with both hands and throttle it. The guys in the first stateroom I came across laughed me out of sight. Only one was in the next room, playing a computer game.

"Check the Nest," he mumbled while he otherwise focused on gunning down digitized Nazis. "They'll have one."

The Nest was the stateroom occupied by the Valkyries, a close-knit gang of female aviators. On *Independence*, women represented one out of five sailors but only one out of maybe fifteen pilots. They were smart and stuck together, a protective measure on a Boat dominated by men.

They also packed an impressive collection of domestic gear, which likely included a vacuum cleaner.

I found their stateroom and knocked.

Athena appeared in the doorway. "What do you want?"

"I..." My thoughts scrambled as a heady scent of citrus shampoos, flowery deodorant, and estrogen poured out in an intoxicating wave of female chemicals.

The vaunted Super Hornet pilot, scourge of the Persian Gulf on prior deployments, wore oversized pink pajamas. The Navy allowed female aviators to wear their hair long, and her blond hair was loose over her shoulders instead of pulled back in its usual warrior braid.

Behind her, the squadron's only Taiwanese-American, Kyra Kao, aka Guns, turned at her desk to fix me with large eyes forming glittering black pools. A pop tune belted from her computer's speakers. Dressed in service khakis, the impressively tall Hawkeye pilot dubbed Amazon applied makeup in front of one of the sink mirrors. Rowdy's horsey face grinned at me from a top bunk, while Medusa glared up at me from the magazine she was reading on her own rack.

They all eyed me while I gaped at them.

They looked a whole lot different in jammies than they did in their baggy flight suits. On a ship where alcohol wasn't allowed, this was as close to buzzed as I could get, being a young man subjected to the lifestyle of a monk and stuck on a ship where men outnumbered women five to one.

I fell in love right then, though not with anybody in particular; they were like a girl band whose members were attractive enough individually but standing all together became dizzying.

Athena snapped her fingers to bring me back to earth. “Let’s go. Spit it out.”

Hoping to recover my professional dignity, I cleared my throat and stood to full height. “I’m wondering if I can borrow a vacuum cleaner for a few minutes.”

She chuckled. “Are you, now?”

The other girls laughed. My face blazed hot.

“And what are you going to do for us, flyboy?”

“What do you want me to do?”

Athena turned. “What should we make him do, Valkyries?”

“Let’s see how many push-ups you can do,” said Amazon. “You game?”

I shrugged. “Make a hole.”

Eyes flashing at this sudden entertainment, they got out of my way as I dropped. Now, I am fully aware this was weird, but being a young peacock, I was all for it. Every young guy with wings thinks he’s God’s gift to women, and I’m ashamed to say I was no exception.

I really went at it, showing off.

“Sound off, nugget!” Rowdy yelled.

“Seven,” I said.

“I can’t hear you!”

“Eight!”

“Like you mean it!”

“Nine! Ten!”

“This idiot is my new front seat,” Kyra said. “He got himself grounded today pissing off the maintenance department.”

“What? You’re my WSO now?” The fun and games forgotten, I sat up. “I hadn’t heard. I’m, uh, glad to be flying with you, Guns. Real glad."

"Wish I could say the same," she said.

I reeled as if struck. "What did *I* do?"

"When you're grounded, *I'm* grounded. I didn't give up nine months of my life for this shit so I could hang out on a boat."

"Okay." I was bewildered. "I'm not really grounded, though." Bryant had made his point and wouldn't mess with the squadron's sortie completion rate.

"Help him out," Amazon said, back to her mascara.

"Sometimes, you have to eat crow to make nice," Athena hinted. "Do you want to fly as bad as you wanted our vacuum cleaner?"

A bell chimed in my thick head as I took her meaning. "I should go make peace with Master Chief Bryant anyway."

"Yes!" Kyra sighed. "Obviously."

Athena offered a mock-impressed smile. "He's not as dumb as he looks."

"Great," Medusa muttered over her magazine. "Is he leaving now?"

"I'll do it right now, Guns," I vowed. "I'll make it right."

Her angry expression softened. "Good. Thanks."

"Hey, Knapp," Athena said.

I turned. "Yes?"

She gave me a handheld vacuum cleaner. "Bring it back in one piece, or we'll break you into pieces. Got it?"

"Yes, ma'am."

Back in the passageway, instead of heading back to my stateroom, I started the journey toward the ship's bow, which required the usual constant navigation past sailors and knee knockers.

Around me, pipes and hidden machinery growled and gurgled. Something in the bowels of the ship clanged. A jet landed on the roof, which as always sounded like a building collapsing.

As the shock shivered down the bulkheads, the captain of the Boat came on the 1MC, and I stopped along with everybody else to listen as he announced it was a fantastic day to be in the Navy and then served up an affirmational anecdote to inspire the crew during its fourteen-hour workday.

By necessity, an aircraft carrier operated at a continuous state of readiness as if America was already at war, which, depending on what part of the world it traveled, it often was. This required a motivated crew that stayed on constant edge and never got sloppy.

Finally, I reached the hangar deck, which the guys who worked the flight deck called the "basement," now crowded with parked jets, spare parts, fuel tanks, and sailors jogging or finding inner peace with yoga. Three stories tall, this cavernous, awe-inspiring space ran about two-thirds of the length of *Independence* and, like most of the carrier, smelled like fuel and grease and humanity.

Tugs lugged their loads. Sailors clambered over a few aircraft, inspecting metal organs and unscrewing plates to yank out handfuls of wire, my Rhino not among them, thank Hermes. Most of these men and women were kids fresh out of high school either having the adventure of their lives or wondering why the hell they'd signed up for this.

The sun glared across the deck through an open

elevator bay. The hangar terminated in open air, offering a view of blue sky and bluer sea.

I found Maintenance Master Chief Bryant writing something down on a clipboard while listening to the petitions of a small crowd of grease monkeys. I waited until they'd left with their orders before I made my move.

"A word, Master Chief?"

He looked up and gave me an evil grin I now knew well. "I was wondering when you might show up. Your bird's got a lot of issues, Lieutenant."

"Yeah, about that, Master Chief. I think if we're both being honest, we'd admit I'm the one with the issues."

I had his full attention now. "Go on. I'm listening."

I took a deep breath and plunged ahead. "I put Sam through unnecessary work because I thought it would give me an edge." That had come out wrong, as I'd intended to blame Duke for everything, but the truth seemed to work just as well, so I stuck with it. "I'll apologize to him personally, but I thought I'd see you first."

The bearish man smiled again before stepping into my personal space, his bulk filling my view. "Do you know what keeps the squadron flying, sir?"

"The maintenance department," I replied dutifully.

He guffawed. "I thought we were being honest! You wanted to say the *aviators* do, and that's fine, but you'd be wrong on both counts. What keeps the squadron flying is *trust*. You trust your crew, and they trust you. Got it?"

"Got it, Master Chief."

"All right," he said. "Like I said, your bird's got a lot of issues, but your crack maintenance department will have it or any other plane you end up flying ready by tomorrow, guaranteed."

I held out my hand. "Thank you, Master Chief."

"It's a fantastic day to be in the Navy." He took my hand in his massive paw and gave it a quick shake. "I probably overreacted. Well, no hard feelings."

I turned to leave, but he called after me. "One last question, if you don't mind."

"What's that?"

"What's with the vacuum cleaner?"

I looked down at it. "To remind me that sometimes, you have to suck it up."

That, and learning a little humility is not a bad thing.

Bryant rumbled with laughter. "Better get used to it, sir. This *is* the Navy."

We didn't part as bosom buddies or anything like that, but we were on solid ground, and my story had one less villain. I was still FNG4 with a long way to go before I'd find my place on this Boat, but within twenty-four hours I'd be flying again, and I'd be able to tell Kyra Kao I'd taken care of a problem she'd gotten stuck sharing. At least a few Gs had been lifted off my shoulders.

Sometimes, it's not the battles you lose, but the ones you win, even the little ones, that truly count. Any landing you walk away from is a win.

SIX

We're getting to the part of the story where I tell you I did something really hotshot on *Independence* to earn my squadron's grudging respect. That my plan finally paid off with me winning accolades, like the cathartic end of an '80s movie about a talented loser maturing to become the mighty hero he was destined to be.

I'd fantasized about it often enough during my chair flying. Spectacular dogfights that thundered across the sky. Tiger waiting on the deck to tell me, *Attaboy, Gargoyle. I believed in you all along. I guess you just had to believe in yourself and become the man you were destined to be.* Kyra Kao falling in love with me on the spot. Duke conceding defeat with a scowl. Pop grinning as he says, *Brother, you can be my wingman anytime.* I lived happily forever after.

Real life is not an '80s action movie, though a young man can always dream.

Oh, I did finally gain everybody's acceptance, more or less, over the next few months as summer bled into fall and *Independence* called on liberty ports in Hawaii and Guam before steaming into the Philippine Sea. That much is accurate.

I didn't do it by being the best, though. I did it by learning my job and by not being a menace to myself and everybody else. I was still a nugget and therefore a natural born screwup, but I'd slowly learned the ropes to a point where my squadron could depend on me.

And that was everything, it turned out. Respect carries far more weight than affection in the military.

When you're hurtling twenty-five thousand feet above the sea in a screaming metal tube loaded with gas and bombs, you want to know the guy next to you isn't going to get you killed. You tend to like the aviator you can depend on with your life, and you only become that pilot through dogged practice, once you realize military aviation is more akin to surgery than swashbuckling.

After four months of flying, I was on the cusp of becoming that guy. In fact, I was finally starting to do my job with style.

In naval aviation, style is everything. It does not mean showing off for attention. It's when you internalize the job to a point where you do it with minimal effort or thought, a confidence broadcasting even in the way you walk onto the flight deck, tell a tale, or eat your chow.

When you possess style, everybody knows you kick ass without you ever having to point it out. A civilian might see arrogance, but out in the Pacific, it was just being a pro.

Once you win respect, you are considered reborn. Your name rings out, only you don't make a name, you receive it. That's how it works with aviators.

On the day of my naming, I marched onto the flight deck with Pop and Kyra Kao for some practice at basic flight maneuvering, or BFM—the Navy's sterilized description for maneuvering used in one-on-one dogfighting.

Helmeted flight crews swarmed the deck. Yellow shirts directing traffic. Brown shirts readying aircraft for flight. Green shirts manning the catapult and arresting gear. Purple shirts pumping gas into aircraft.

Blue shirts towing planes back and forth from the hangar elevators with yellow tractors. Red shirts mounting and arming bombs. White shirts observing for quality control and safety.

The sensory assault began the instant I stepped onto the deck. Metallic screams and clacks, engine roars, grease all over everything, fuel and oil stink, waves of hot exhaust and steam, and a perpetual stiff, briny wind blowing off a rolling sea that glowed under the radiant sky.

As I said before, it's a violent place, but to me, the flight deck was a beautiful ballet and orchestra, all of it devoted to a single wonderful purpose, which was getting me airborne and welcoming me home.

Holly Young, the usual brown shirt, delivered a salute and status update on my Rhino's preflight condition. Geared up and with thirty minutes to go before takeoff, Kyra and I circled the plane for our hands-on inspection and then mounted the boarding ladders to nestle into our cockpits.

I plugged into the oxygen supply, made small talk with Sam while I buckled up, and strapped my boards onto my thighs, which contained my operation crib sheet and where I'd track my fuel level and number of minutes I had left in the air. The bullet-proof canopy connected with the fuselage and enclosed us in our little Plexiglas bubble.

"Don't disappoint me, Knapp," Kyra said behind me.

She wanted us to outsmart Pop this time and knock him out of the sky in our mock dogfight. From her lips to God's ears. Pop was way better than me. A centurion with more than a hundred carrier landings under his belt, he was our operations officer, resident combat instructor, and Achilles all rolled into one man.

Kyra activated the intercom. “I said—”

“I heard you, Guns.” I turned on the APU and fired the engines in sequence. The air filled with a breathy roar like I’d switched on the world’s biggest vacuum cleaner.

“You know, sometimes, I think you try too hard,” she said.

I jerked my head toward the backseat. “I do? What do you mean?”

“Trying to impress everybody.”

I chewed on this criticism. “Oh.”

“This time, I want you to try as hard as you can.”

“Roger that.” I raised my hand to give her a thumbs-up.

Working with her had required some adjustment, but over time, she’d shown me what a good WSO could do. All aerial fighting is fought in the future—maneuvering against a moving adversary so that at a future point in time you’ll be in the zone for a kill shot—but a good WSO thinks of everything, keeping track of the big picture while the pilot becomes immersed in the fight.

Besides all that, she’d turned out to be a friend, always giving me simple, practical advice from a perspective outside the testosterone-fueled game of aviator competition. Whenever I boresighted on the bullshit, she set me straight.

The ground crew signaled each other in their unique sign language and watched everything like hungry hawks except for my jet, which they regarded warily as if it were a giant monster barely under their control. They crouched and maneuvered to work and see and avoid getting inadvertently crushed, speared, or barbecued.

Their work done, Sam finally turned me over to a yellow shirt. Tummy swirling with dogfighting butterflies, I taxied into position on the catapult. *Independence* steamed on a straight track into the wind, which would lend our jet another twenty knots of lift to get us airborne.

"Jet blast deflector is up," Kyra said.

I opened the throttles. The engines' pitch changed as they ramped to full power. The jet's burner cans flared. Wings spread, the jet trembled under tension, a bullet in a cocked gun. The small crowd of airmen bristled with raised thumbs. At the conclusion of a dense list of routine procedures, we were finally good to go.

I offered a crisp salute to the catapult officer and settled my helmeted head against the seat rest. My left hand stayed on the throttles while my right grabbed the towel rack on the canopy bow, kept out of the way until I needed it.

A green shirt on the deck took a knee, touched the deck with one hand, and pointed down the runway with the other. The gesture always struck me as melodramatic, and I imagined him crying: *Hark, brave knight of the air! Onward, to the sport of the angels!*

Enclosed in a transparent protective bubble, the catapult officer pressed his FIRE button.

Onward—

In an instant, we roared toward the edge of the world on more than thirty thousand pounds of thrust while the tripling G force shoved my oxygen mask against my face and my body flooded with adrenaline and endorphins. Bouncing in my harness, I pushed the throttles past full power.

The Super Hornet raced down the track. Through it all, I grinned like a maniac, trembling with excitement.

Then our wheels left the deck with a whiplash thump as we vaulted from the bow, shot off like a ball from the world's biggest pinball machine. Behind me, the catapult shuttle slammed into the brake with a *boom*.

The launch had taken only two and a half seconds.

The G forces pancaking me against my seat faded, and I grabbed the stick to take control of the jet. The sea rushed under me a hundred feet below. Then the miracle of flight occurred, and we were aloft and bound for the heavens.

I made a righthand clearing turn, raised my gear and flaps, and turned left until I was flying parallel with the Boat.

In accordance with the mission plan, I brought us up through a clump of cottony cumulus to rendezvous with my flight lead. I was insanely happy to be flying. Imagine you're driving a car, only this car is twenty thousand feet above the ocean and traveling at six hundred miles an hour.

This high up, barreling through a clean sky over an azure Pacific with great visibility horizon to horizon, you feel like you're touching the Grail.

My bowels rumbled.

As feared, the cabin pressurization made me gassy, no big deal when you're by yourself or with a dude like Duke in the backseat but a far different story when flying with a little firecracker you have a crush on.

If it was Duke, I would have splattered the canopy with the sound, but it being Kyra, I raised a cheek to let go in a slow hydraulic hiss.

Unfortunately, I couldn't disguise the stench of digesting wardroom burrito cut with pure brimstone. I smelled it even with my oxygen mask on.

Kyra sniffed. "Ugh."

I hung my head. "Yeah."

"Sorry, Knapp. I couldn't hold it."

"It's all good, lady," I said, thanking my lucky stars she'd let one go too.

I brought my jet a quarter of a mile abeam of Pop's left wing and locked into tactical formation. During the day, we tried to keep the comms clear, so I gave him a simple thumbs up that said, *Lead, I'm visual and as fragged.*

He signaled me back. *Stand by to tango.*

Roger that.

"Check tapes on HUD," Pop called on the radio, referring to the cockpit's heads-up display.

"Tapes," I replied.

"Fight's on."

"Fight's on."

I lit the cans as I banked onto my right wing, eyes glued on the dot of Pop's plane circling the other way. I leveled out on track for a rapid head-on merge. After a right-to-right pass, we'd break and simulate trying to shoot each other down.

"Let's kick his ass," Kyra said.

"We're gonna light him up," I vowed to the sky goddess behind me.

"We'd better, or I'll make you do more push-ups."

BFM practice was all about improving one's ability to solve range, angle, and closure problems to either gain or deny position for shooting. After the pass, I'd try to get behind his 3/9 line—in simpler terms, I wanted him in front of me instead of behind.

Once there, I'd dog him until we gained a radar lock in my weapons envelope, and then I'd count coup. If Pop got on my six instead, my main job was to create problems for him by eliminating turning room or finding a way out of the fight.

All of this required split-second observation, prediction, and reaction. Calling on all the chair flying I'd done against my imaginary North Korean adversaries, I put on my war face.

I was ready to put a hurt on Pop.

LOL.

Remember what I said about me not doing anything particularly astounding that earned eternal admiration and accolades from my peers? What happened next was Pop destroyed us while he recorded the whole thing as a snuff film for our later debrief.

I've endured enough humiliation so far in this modest memoir, so I'll skip the gory details. Suffice to say he was the more experienced aviator, faster on the draw in decision making, and had a natural feel for how hard he could push his aircraft.

What I can tell you with some pride, though, is I made him work hard for his glory, and if he was half as sweaty and strung out as I was by the time we ran low on fuel and playtime was over, I'd accomplished a mighty feat.

"Next time, you cocky bastard," Kyra swore.

"We'll get him next time," I agreed.

"I'm ladder," Pop radioed, informing us he was on

the flight schedule to land.

It was time to RTB, or return to base.

We entered the pattern, found our interval, and eventually made our way into the overhead break. Worn out and beaten up by our jousting, my subsequent thump of a landing hardly resembled a textbook.

"You did real good," Kyra said. "You get better every time."

I folded the wings and started to taxi. "Not as good as Pop."

"Dude. He's TOPGUN." She'd never really expected us to best him.

"I wonder how good the North Koreans are," I said.

"Not very. Their planes suck too. The Chinese, though. They'd be tough."

I snorted. Even then, we had no inkling we were on a collision course with a shooting war against the People's Republic of China, or PRC. We'd been briefed on the upcoming Taiwanese election, as one of the candidates, Chao Akemi, was running on a platform of declaring independence, which might trigger war between these countries.

She was behind in the polls, however, so we didn't give it much thought. At the time, instead of worrying about war, we were all looking forward to dropping anchor at Busan during our official visit to South Korea.

"Anyway," Kyra said, "you know how Pop got his call sign? He forgot to release the emergency brake before he launched at the cat."

"What? Really?"

"Yup." She burst into laughter. "Talk about burning rubber."

"Huh." I didn't know that. I'd always assumed it was because he was so good with the Vulcan cannon or something.

"And you know Sparky? He earned his call sign because he boltered four times while trying to do a nighttime landing during a storm."

"Wow."

"And Dangle's another funny story. He ejected on deck, and his parachute got caught in the antennae. They had to cut him down."

"Huh." I wanted to ask her how she got hers but wisely thought better of it.

"The moral is even the great aviators start out as nuggets."

We headed below to meet up with Pop. In the ready room, we'd watch the HUD tapes of our BFM encounters while Pop offered constructive criticism from notes he'd scrawled on one of his thigh boards. Normally, I was pretty gung-ho for this sort of interaction with a senior aviator showing me the ropes, but I was feeling a little uncertain.

I told you I was growing into the job. I never said I stopped wanting to be the best at it. While I was in a sense competing with everybody else, my biggest opponent remained the guy I saw in the mirror, both the idealized guy I wanted to be, as well as the guy who still thought deep down he was the same screwup from York, Maryland and would never truly make the cut.

I flew with the best but still sometimes felt like an imposter.

The Navy was a big, bloated mother who gave you toys, smacked you around, and loved but often ignored you. *Be all that you can be*, like the Army claimed, had an air of truth in the Navy, but another slogan might be, *The Navy, it's whatever you want it to be.* You can treat it as a job, a waystation to something better, or an almost religious higher calling, and I'm not embarrassed to say I'm one of the higher calling types.

More than that, I'd interpreted its slogan as: *The Navy: be somebody else.* Somebody I'd always wanted to be. But I had to earn it first.

We descended to the ready room, where I stopped in surprise at the sight of the entire squadron grinning back at me.

Pepsi Man stood from his leather chair and raised his hand. "XO! If I may..."

"By all means," the executive officer said, giving him the floor.

"I have had the pleasure of sharing one naval domicile with the unfortunate nugget standing before us, and I have found him to be a true Gargoyle who takes his licks, never overlooks an opportunity to excel, and demonstrates aptitude with vacuuming," the aviator proclaimed. "He also cantered all the way to the plumbing department to search and rescue our TOPGUN wrench. I hereby endorse him to the call sign review board."

"Hear, hear!" the aviators cried, seconding the motion.

Pop patted my shoulder while I stood there stunned. "We'll debrief later." Wearing an amused half-smile, he tilted his head toward the doorway. "Now get back out there and wait while we figure out what to christen you."

"I'll do what I can to get you a good one," Kyra assured me.

Still too stunned to speak, I went back outside, where I heard the muffled roar of laughter as the aviators shared stories of my embarrassing exploits, fantastic failings, and myriad mistakes.

I started to pace, as the call sign they gave me would follow me around for life as both a badge and something of a scarlet letter. Sometimes flashy, usually embarrassing, call signs have provided a source of chagrin and icebreaking stories since they were invented.

To pass the time while I waited, I tried to guess what the squadron would come up with for me. In some cases, your call sign makes an obvious play on your name, appearance, or some peculiar mannerism. A gal with red hair might be renamed Red, a guy named Rod Hind could end up either Hot Rod or Frumby, a guy or gal sporting a heavy Southern drawl might be christened Bubba.

I considered how they'd play it in my case. My last name of Knapp was problematic. I'd probably end up stuck with *Cat* or *Wet*. Worse, I might end up with something like *SNAP* or *Vacuum Man*. I was starting to soak in flop sweat. I was more nervous than my first carrier-qualification landing and even my first nighttime carrier landing, which is saying something.

As if responding to my thoughts, loud cheering sounded from the room. The squadron had chosen a name for me by acclamation.

The door opened to reveal the XO. "Get in here, Knapp."

I followed him inside to face the music.

"Listen up, Gargoyles," he said. "This is apparently one remarkable aviator, as I don't remember hearing so many outstanding candidates for call signs.

One thing they all have in common is conveying how hard this kid tries to be good, how he never gives up, and how well he sucks it up when he falls on his ass. If there's one thing we all know about Jack Knapp, it's he's one eager beaver. And so, ladies and gentlemen and Gargoyles, I am pleased to present: *Beaver*."

A tiny part of me had held out hope for something cool like Jackhammer or Scorpion or, yes, God be praised, even Maverick, but Beaver…wasn't terrible.

The best part? I was FNG4 no longer. It really was like being reborn.

Beaver. Yup, that was me.

I grinned. "Thank you, sir."

The entire squadron formed a receiving line to shake my hand and welcome Beaver to the Gargoyles, as if they were meeting me for the first time and this time as a peer, not as an FNG.

Morrison was first, offering a hearty, "Good job, amigo." Even Tiger gave me a shake and said, "Do us proud, Beaver," while Duke delivered a seemingly sincere, "Well done, man."

I was officially in their tribe now. Yes, many of them had given me a hard time, and while I liked and respected some on a personal level, it's true I didn't like others so much. Thanks to movies, many civilians seem to think guys in the service are all diehard bros earnestly yelling *hooah!*, but the truth is most of the people you serve with are somewhere on a sliding scale between co-workers and the more annoying members of your family.

Relating to them through the tribe, however, is different. In that context, we would die for each other.

When I think about these aviators now, the ones

who survived and the many who didn't, I feel only a powerful and primitive love.

SEVEN

After my first day standing trial before the Tribunal of the Special Court, convened by the Fourteenth National People's Congress under the Supreme People's Court of China, you, Deputy Bureau Chief Zhang, asked me what I thought of justice in the People's Republic.

I said I'd have to get back to you on that, as I hadn't encountered any yet.

This struck you as hilarious.

When in session, it certainly has the trappings of a trial, with me seated in a dock—basically a wooden cage—with blue-uniformed bailiffs in peaked caps standing at stiff attention behind me, judges scowling on benches in front of me, and a very large peanut gallery. After an endless series of speeches and procedures, a prosecutor yelled a lot while the spectators groaned.

But it isn't justice. It's a show trial, and I told you so.

We were strolling through the courtyard, which at Qincheng Prison is sectioned off by high brick walls so the prisoners can't see or talk to each other during their daily or weekly exercise. As a high-ranking prisoner, I'm allowed an hour a day.

You gave me an indulgent smile. "Of course. Your guilt is pre-ordained."

I would be found guilty of made-up war crimes.

While I hadn't really expected any other outcome for the trial, I was still stunned by the news. "Is anything about your country real?"

You lit a cigarette and offered me one. You smoke Zhonghua brand, favored by top Party officials. The cigarette made me think of cancer, firing squads, and the time your guards burned me with one, but I took it anyway and accepted your gracious offer of a light. As it was my first, I coughed on it.

"Yin and yang," you explained.

The last thing I'd expected a hardened intelligence officer to talk about is Chinese cosmology, but you plowed ahead as if this were a natural topic. Despite the big black-rimmed glasses that good-looking people in the States only sport when they're trying to be ironic, you wear expensive suits and carry yourself more like a Wall Street trader who just bagged an elephant than a Party apparatchik.

I blinked at the nicotine rush. "Which means what?"

"Dark and light, negative and positive, passive and active, disorder and order, each in conflict yet dependent on the other to form a constantly changing whole. Chaos creates energy, which gives rise to harmonious order in cycles. Rise to joyous *unity*. As it is in the universe, so it is in social organization." You paused to take an affected drag on your cigarette. "The trial will stimulate cathartic renewal by fulfilling its role as People's theater."

So there it was. Your side lost and China is under blockade, and now your people are jobless and hungry and you think a handy scapegoat will fix your problems. In an enlightened country like yours, there's nothing like a live TV execution to unite the people against a common foe and save a little face.

"I'm the bad guy," I said. "I'm yin."

"You are America. America is yin. Last dregs of old century yielding to bright energy of future. Dying American eagle in struggle with rising Chinese dragon."

I reminded you the American eagle delivered a whole lot of whoop ass on the Chinese dragon during the war.

"As usual, your thought is not correct, Prisoner 2299," you pontificated. "America has the attention of a housefly. It thinks through a lens of half-hour TV programs. China thinks in terms of dialectical materialism played over centuries. Taipei's declaration of independence forced us to act prematurely, risk that proved a woeful mistake but rich in profound insights. China's struggle is eternal. Your century is in twilight, ours in golden dawn. When appropriate, the war will end, but our struggle cannot."

"Okay." I wanted to get back to the part where I was a war criminal.

"You will be found guilty, Prisoner 2299. The penalty is death."

"Oh." I took a final long drag on my cig until I was sucking filter.

"The court may be convinced toward leniency," you said. "A death sentence, but with a reprieve."

I caught on quick. "If I do what, exactly?"

"I do not know." You pretended to enter a state of deep thought on my behalf. "Perhaps you write a confession and read it on television for the world to see."

"Why bother?" Exposure to the bullshit of the Chinese Communist Party was a form of psychological torture on its own. "It's all a sham. Why not write it yourself and say I wrote it?"

You blew a stream of silver smoke. "We prefer to edit."

I stood accused of blowing up a hospital ship and was to confess to doing it. I was to say the commander of my air wing ordered it. I would name three of my comrades as accomplices in the act. To soften the blow, you said I could pick dead men, as taking part in the People's theater wouldn't matter to them. They were just names now, existing only in memory.

I said, "Jack Knapp, Lieutenant, junior-grade, serial number—"

Saying this usually triggered a sharp call for the guards, but this time you just waved your hand. "Think on it. You can earn your life. And the pain will stop."

You brought me back to my cell, cheerfully explaining to me how it was once occupied by a brutal Nationalist general who'd killed thousands, as if this bit of trivia would fascinate me. You left without getting my answer. You already felt confident I would play along, which I found vaguely insulting, though yeah, I certainly do want to go on living.

After the second day of the trial ended in boredom and terror, the door cranked open, and I expected another brutal round of random, pointless questions about the hospital ship while stone-faced guards worked me over. Instead, the guards brought in a typewriter, ream of paper, spare ribbon, and bottle of Wite-Out.

I resisted at first, but the typewriter seemed to call to me. The code of conduct is pretty specific about not betraying your country, and it required me to give only my name, rank, and serial number. I thought about typing it out a thousand times just to have something to do, even though it'd mean a thousand more beatings.

On the other hand, I don't want to be executed. At times like this, it becomes far less theoretical and a very real choice about what you're willing to die for.

In the end, I reasoned that as long as my life was passing before my eyes at the threat of execution, I should put my Academy English degree to good use and write it all down. Being a dumb nugget? I can confess to that all day. I discovered that as long as I gave you pages, the torture stopped. So I started typing as if life and limb depended on it, as if this were a very real replay of *One Thousand and One Nights*.

While my life in fact does in fact depend on it, so far I've written everything except what you wanted, comrade. This is probably the longest ongoing confession you've ever seen. You made a simple request to this barbarian American capitalist running dog to write a confession to war crimes, and he's giving you everything but, without even the satisfaction of learning juicy military intel you couldn't already pull from Google.

"My heart soars at your progress," you often say, sounding like the Southern belle giving me a smiley *Bless your heart* when she means, *You're a special kind of stupid.* "But now you must arrive at sinking of the hospital ship."

Deluding myself you were indulging me maybe out of enjoyment and that I'd won over my first fan as a writer, I asked you, "So what do you think of it so far?"

You shrugged. "The dragon flies, and the phoenix dances."

I wasn't sure what this meant. Your tone didn't sound very laudatory.

That's fine. In the end, it doesn't matter to me what

you think.

Surely, Deputy Bureau Chief Zhang, by now you must have realized I'm not writing this for you.

EIGHT

The first rumors of war arrived in a briefing.

I awoke in my rack sweating and parched as usual after sleeping under the hot catapult track. After months of sailing around the Pacific, I was so used to the shuddering crashes of aircraft pounding the roof I couldn't sleep without it.

The phone was ringing.

I hopped down onto the deck to answer it. At the other end, the duty officer told me the squadron's officers had been ordered to muster in the ready room.

After I hung up, I said, "Reveille, you guys."

Aviators stayed up late and slept late almost as a rule. I'd twiddled my thumbs on alert status from 0200 to 0400, and I'd planned to sleep in too.

My watch sneered 0800.

Pepsi Man, Duke, Dangle, Track, and Morrison—now call sign Snoopy in honor of all the earnest chair flying he did—kept on snoring.

I grabbed one of my shoes and banged it against the bunk frame. "Rise and shine, America's finest!"

"Go to hell," Dangle said from his rack.

"The skipper wants us all in the ready room pronto for an all officers' meeting."

While the men stirred and cursed my rural Maryland lineage, I reached into the medicine cabinet for my toothbrush to start my morning ritual. Spitting into the sink after a good gargle, I put my brush away and lathered up to shave.

"Damn, Beaver," said Duke as he heaved himself

groaning into a sitting position. "When you fly commercial, do you sit there in coach the whole time praying the pilot has a heart attack?"

I ran my razor across my uneven, wispy stubble. "Why would I do that?"

"So the flight attendants will get on the PA and ask if anybody aboard knows how to fly a plane, of course. Then you can run up the aisle and be the hero."

"Somebody has to answer the phone around here," I said.

"You probably dreamed it," Track said, still in his bunk. He pulled his blanket over his head. "There's no meeting. You dreamed the whole thing."

"That explains why your mom was in my rack." I splashed hot water over my face and toweled off, and then started combing my short hair with my fingers.

The aviators chuckled without mirth. After six months at sea, we were all sick of it and each other, the way rats packed in a cage inevitably gnaw each other's tails off. The stress of constant flying battered our necks and lumbars. The daily diet of G forces many times our weight took its toll. The noise and hazards and stupidity and bland food and oily stink grew steadily more grating. The long isolation from the real world with only carefully worded emails, occasional satellite calls, and restricted, very slow internet added to the stress.

The carrier was starting to feel less like a warship and more like jail. Thankfully, *Independence* would soon drop anchor at Busan. We were all looking forward to blowing off steam during our well-deserved liberty.

Busan was about to party.

Honestly, I didn't mind the hardships as much as the others. While I'd found my way, I was still a nugget, and even the suffering was a novel adventure for me. I actually regarded it and the world-weary bitching I'd earned as an exciting rite of passage.

Nonetheless, I was looking forward to our port call. *Independence* had made six stops at liberty ports during the deployment so far, and true to my call sign and to bank my pay, I'd stayed aboard each time. I'd even volunteered as boat officer for two stops, taking responsibility for ferrying drunken sailors on a bobbing boat from land back to the carrier.

Not this time, though. Not Busan.

Why, you ask? Dude! I was going to freaking South Korea!

Let me tell you something about war: You travel. Which is why God invented war, according to comedian Paul Rodriguez: so Americans learn geography. I was utterly stoked about the prospect of visiting a foreign land, which would be a new experience for me.

In Busan, after the joint exercises and obligatory cultural exchanges, I'd check out some street markets and Buddhist temples, eat a lot of crazy food, get my drink on, and try to forget the Navy for a while.

More importantly, I had another tasking on Korean soil. A covert operation. Top secret and high stakes, requiring my A game.

What could this secret mission be? To spend some quality time with Lieutenant Kyra Kao, of course. Just the two of us on a real date in civilian clothes and no third-wheel peanut gallery.

We'd been "dating," kind of, for a while now, at least in my imagination and as far as it's allowed in the

Navy, which is to say with no touching and almost zero privacy. Even in the air, we weren't really alone, and besides that, there's no Mile High Club when it comes to supersonic fighter jets, though the gung-ho will tell you flying one is the most fun you can have with your pants on.

That's not to say sex doesn't happen on aircraft carriers. Far from it. Lucky sailors find a way to get naked in closets, ventilation spaces, maintenance areas, and every other nook and cranny on the ship.

Kyra and I didn't. We didn't put a name on what was happening and I wasn't even sure it was real, but we spent a lot of time together, from dining in the wardroom to watching movies in the ready room after flight ops with a regulation distance of one foot separating us.

I had a room booked at a hotel in Busan that was pretty fancy by my meager standards, where I hoped to take things to the next level.

Right now, though, I was still in my stateroom pulling on my brown aviator boots and waiting for my roommates to get their act together, unaware that an unthinkable war was already brewing that would ruin my romantic plans.

After some time getting ready and casually stomping on each other's last nerve, we filed out into the passageway looking more or less presentable in our flight suits.

We found the ready room filled with aviators, most of them crowded around the coffee urn. I wanted in on that, but first I had some detective work to do.

I inspected the boards. Nothing odd about the flight schedule, nobody conspicuous was missing, and the crowd buzzed with questions not gossip.

I knew just who to ask to get the scuttlebutt.

"Hey, Pop," I said. "What's the word?"

The operations officer turned thoughtful. "My guess? Shore leave is canceled."

I chuckled at his bad joke, filled a mug with coffee, and took my seat between Snoopy and a pilot called Frog, who'd earned his call sign on account of his breathy, raspy voice. Tiger surveyed all of us with his back against the wall, muscular arms folded over his barrel chest.

"I'll bet it's nothing," Frog croaked.

"Another PowerPoint presentation," Snoopy groaned.

"Worse. Some kind of kumbaya—"

The XO walked onstage and raised his hands for quiet. "Listen up!"

Aviator boil fell to a simmer as a score of conversations trailed off.

He said, "Okay, ready for this? Mother's upcoming port call is canceled."

You can imagine the collective groan that ensued upon hearing that. Somebody crumpled paper behind me, and I wondered if the XO was about to be stoned.

I groaned louder than most as I watched my big plans flame out of the sky.

"Settle down," the XO said. "This is important."

Tiger stepped away from the wall, and the rowdy aviators instantly silenced.

"Here's the deal," the skipper declared. "Taiwan's election returns came in overnight, and they called it. Chao Akemi won the national election."

The room filled with excited murmurs. We all

knew what that meant.

While at sea, aviators attend briefs covering everything from tactics to geopolitics. For example, we were steaming near the Ryukyu Islands now, a chain extending from the Japanese islands to Taiwan. We'd learned that China recognized Japan's control of the islands until oil was discovered in the 1970s, around which time China changed its tune about who owned what islands. The Treaty of Mutual Cooperation and Security required America to fight alongside Japan if the People's Republic ever seized some of them.

We'd also learned about China's claims in the South China Sea. A third of maritime trade sails through this stretch of water, four trillion bucks of it every year, in fact. Every country surrounding these waters has competing claims, craving access to energy buried in the seabed and strategic control of the shipping lanes. China went so far as to build and militarize artificial islands in an attempt to assert control. The Navy frequently exercised freedom of navigation through the area, their intrepid crews thumbing their noses at China the whole way.

In a region of potential flashpoints, though, none proved as dangerous as Taiwan, which brings me back to President-Elect Chao Akemi.

At the time, most Americans had no idea how dangerous her election was or why.

After WW2 ended with the fall of Japan, Mao Zedong and his communists went back to trying to overthrow the nationalist government, largely succeeding by 1949, when they founded the People's Republic of China, or PRC. Two million mainlanders fled to the island of Taiwan, which held out against the communists.

For a while, the free world recognized Taiwan as the legitimate government of China, but that changed in 1972 with President Nixon's new China policy, and the PRC replaced Taiwan in the United Nations.

The PRC always considered Taiwan a rogue province—Chinese Tapei—and believed they'd reunify via peaceful means and, barring that, using intimidation and force. China's military buildup, doctrine, and training was all about making this happen, despite decades of appeasement.

As for us, the 1979 Taiwan Relations Act said we'd kinda sorta maybe defend the island from invasion, ambiguity designed to keep the PRC from invading but also deter Taiwan from declaring independence and triggering a war that America needed like a hole in the head.

In short, it was a powder keg, proof wars often leave hot messes that result in the next war.

"Now it's time for some fresh intel," Tiger said. "Lieutenant Danby?"

The aviators stirred at the mention of the intelligence officer assigned to VFA-95. Lieutenant Elizabeth Danby, she of the iron-clad, shiny-white smile and ever-sunny disposition that lit up this dull, utilitarian room decorated with competition, martial history, and gray piping.

Once, the guys had acted as obtuse as possible to try to crack that legendary disposition but failed. In truth, their hearts hadn't been in it. They liked her the way she was. Danby was simply nice to have around during mission planning, even if the intel she served hot often included everything except what you needed to know.

She stood and gave the room a sweeping wave. "Good morning, y'all! Now here's the word of the day."

She backed up toward a map appearing on the projection screen, the XO barely scuttling out of the way in time. The lights dimmed. "Right now, the PLAN is conducting exercises off the coast of Taiwan." PLAN: the People's Liberation Army Navy. "Exercises simulating an island invasion and all that? Figuring it'd intimidate the Taiwanese? Well, it backfired on them something spectacular. Taiwan just elected a president who promised to declare independence once and for good. So things have gotten real interesting. We know there's a big PLA buildup in Fujian Province right here." Ground forces.

She traced a circle on the map with her index finger. At the shortest distance across the Taiwan Strait, Fujian is only eighty miles from Taiwan. "If Taiwan does declare independence? We can sure as Shinola expect some form of aggressive PRC response. Anything from a blockade to an all-out shooting war."

Then she stood there smiling while we gaped back at her in stunned wonder at just how bad things could get in a very short time.

"Thank you, Lieutenant," the XO said as Tiger reclaimed the stage.

The skipper tapped the map. "We're here at the mouth of the East China Sea, about two hundred fifty miles from Busan. We've been ordered to a new station three hundred miles east of Taiwan. The Boat is turning around so we can scoot down with the Ryukyus westward as a screen." The Japanese maintained antiair and antimissile bases on the islands. "We'll be on station by tomorrow night. Once we are, what we will do is observe and wait and show our fist so the Chinese don't do anything stupid. What we will *not* do is start World War Three. Consider that a standing order. Understand?"

We growled our assent.

"Our posture will be defensive, our attitude vigilant," he wrapped up. "From here on out, consider yourself in the lion's den, but just remember we're the lion tamers. Dismissed."

The aviators stood to leave with far more quiet and introspection than they'd arrived with, the usual chips on their shoulders forgotten. I stayed in my chair simply trying to absorb what had happened.

An international crisis had just kicked into high gear.

If war broke out and America was either pushed or pulled into it, I'd be on the front line within range of thousands of Chinese missiles. The United States had good air assets at bases throughout the region, but the Chinese would focus on Guam and our carriers.

The United States had three in the Pacific at the time; *Ronald Reagan* was at Yokosuka getting refitted, and *Theodore Roosevelt* was at Pearl.

For now, *Independence* was on her own.

I'm not ashamed to admit a part of me was scared it might happen, but God help me, I am a little ashamed to confess a part of me hoped it *would* happen.

And it was happening, all right.

We didn't know it at the time, but the lights had already gone out in Taiwan.

NINE

In war, most of the time, you hardly have a clue what's actually going on.

That "fog of war" you hear about is more or less permanent, at least when you're at my pay grade.

Such was the case as *Independence* arrived on station east of Taiwan at the end of March. A cyberattack on Taiwan's electrical grid wreaked havoc on the island, and the Chinese Navy, which had put to sea for military exercises, had encircled it and was enforcing an exclusion zone and harassing shipping.

In case that wasn't heard loud and clear in Tapei, the People's rocket forces fired a few missiles into the Taiwan Strait and bombed Kinmen, part of a chain of small islands serving as Taiwan's first line of defense from amphibious invasion.

We were not invited to the party.

A carrier and its strike group now stood between us and Taiwan. It was *Hunan*, Lieutenant Danby cheerfully informed us, seventy thousand tons fully loaded and built from an old Soviet design with a distinctive curved bow that served as a ski jump to get its planes into the air. The flattop carried forty-four aircraft, including squadrons of fourth-generation Shenyang J-15 Flying Sharks.

That much was known. The rest had all of us aviators speculating 24/7.

In the Dirty Shirt wardroom, we congregated for shared gossip and speculation. This was my favorite wardroom, as it was near our ready room and had a similar menu and the exact same formality as a Denny's, with diners allowed to wear jerseys and flight suits. Aviators often came here for "midrats," or midnight rations, before or after a night launch. After landing in the dark, it was a great place to unwind before hitting the rack.

The menu was limited, at this hour mostly consisting of leftovers along with hamburgers and eggs, that sort of thing. While the ship pitched and rolled on heavy seas, I grabbed a slider with cheese and an egg on top, while Kyra Kao put together a salad.

This done, we set our trays down on one of the tables claimed by the Gargoyles, joining a group of aviators going on or coming off alert status. Immediately, my tray started to slide across the table toward Pepsi Man's lap. I arrested it in time while he continued to hold forth with his expert analysis on what we were doing here.

"This is not the first time China assumed an intimidation posture on Taiwan," he said, as usual speaking like he stepped out of some madman's idea of a Navy manual. "Back in 1996, Taiwan executed its first presidential election, and the Chinese endeavored to become unruly. Clinton force-allocated two carriers to the region, China shit rice, and that was that."

This was the most popular theory among the aviators. Despite the stadium roar of smack talk on the Boat, we all kind of figured this was how the crisis would play out. America would strut up, pull out its big wiener and wave it around, and China would retract back into its shell in terror to ponder Confucius.

"Too bad," Snoopy said. "It'd do them some good to get their asses kicked."

"Careful what you wish for," said Dangle, who'd flown combat missions in the Middle East before coming over to the Pacific. "If we allow Taiwanese merchants to sail under American colors, things could get interesting real quick."

"Where have you guys been?" Rowdy said at the end of the table at her indoor volume, which is to say she was shouting. "Back in '96, China barely even had a floating navy. Now they got a military that could put a real hurt on us. They got satellites watchin' our every move. And here we are, a sittin' duck!"

Everybody growled at the reality check. The truth was the Chinese weren't backing down in the face of American might and strongly worded protest. The Boat was at Condition 3, a state of wartime readiness with about half its weapons manned and armed. When we sortied, we took off with a full loadout of weapons.

We weren't at war, but we had to act even more like we were in case it suddenly arrived.

Otherwise, however, we did little to disguise our presence, sailing exposed within range of a whole lot of missiles, including the DF-21, the dreaded carrier buster. If we were close to hostilities, normally we'd conceal ourselves by giving another ship a carrier signature to use it as a decoy and otherwise shifting into a heightened EMCON condition, where we stopped using radar and radio.

Instead, we were advertising the fact we were here, trying to make a diplomatic statement.

As far as we were concerned at our level of awareness, it was all a massive risk without accomplishing much. We were starting to feel like bait. We'd steam toward Taiwan as if ready to assert our right to the seas, and then somebody would remember a PLAN aircraft carrier stood in our way, and we'd lose another game of chicken.

I sensed politicians and admirals yelling at each other back in Washington over what the next move should be, debating whether Taiwan was worth going to war and calculating how much martial strength could be expressed without starting a war they didn't want to fight.

"Sittin' duck!" Rowdy happily crowed.

"Give it a rest," Dangle said.

"The otherwise able lieutenant is operating under a propaganda-induced misapprehension," Pepsi Man observed with a tsk. "The PRC is a paper dragon. They are not a true peer competitor."

Rowdy guffawed, showing us all her half-chewed food. "Yeah, they are!"

"Their military is green," Dangle argued. "Most of Mother's aviators have combat experience."

"Not feet wet in deep water, they don't. Bombing terrorists in the Sandbox don't count for this kind of fight."

"And all their big, scary missiles?" Dangle scoffed. "They're barely tested."

Rowdy raised her index finger while she chewed. "All it takes is one!"

He shook his head in irritation, no doubt wondering why he was arguing with her. The trays went into a slide to port as the Boat rolled on another swell.

"The lieutenant appears to be campaigning to replace Beaver as morale officer," Pepsi Man said. "Save us, Beaver. Defend your title."

"Leave me out of it." Half my attention was on

the nearby TV mounted in the corner, its channel set to the PLAT. Outside, wind lashed the flight deck with a fine spray. I hoped the Alert 7 wouldn't have to launch while I was manning it.

Intercepting an intruder in that pitch-black soup would be bad enough, but landing on the rolling deck afterwards promised a lifetime of nightmares.

"What do you think, Guns?" Snoopy asked.

Kyra shrugged. "I don't know, but I doubt it'd be a cakewalk."

"I mean about what the PRC is thinking."

"How would I know?"

"I thought you might have an inside track because, you know…"

She bristled. "I know *what*? Spit it out."

"Nothing!" Snoopy raised his hands in surrender. "Forget it."

Guns stood. I'd spent enough time with my little firecracker to know when her fuse was good and lit. "Let's go, Beaver."

"Roger that." I grabbed my tray. "Catch you later, Snoop."

"Yeah." He hunched his shoulders as if trying to disappear. "See ya, amigo."

Dangle checked the time on the PLAT monitor. "We should go too, Rowdy."

"Aye, aye!" She crammed as much greasy slider into her mouth as she could and got to her feet, cheeks bulging.

They made an odd pair. Him reserved and straight-laced, her sharing whatever truth popped into her head at top volume. You'd think this would lead to a different kind of war, but they not only tolerated but complemented each other. In the air, they presented a competent team, a very lethal old married couple.

Dangle led the way to the ready room and paraloft, where we donned our flight gear. From there, we headed outboard through a dim, red-lit catwalk terminating in a ladder that would take us to the flight deck.

I really, really hoped we didn't have to fly tonight.

Independence maintained alert fighters on standby in case it came under a threat that needed to be engaged before it came within range of the enemy's weaponry. The fastest responders were the Alert 7 fighters, which could be airborne in seven minutes.

This necessitated fully briefed aviators sitting in the ready room or—due to the higher present possibility of hostilities—asses parked in fully fueled, preflighted jets. If *Hunan* launched a surprise attack on this ungodly night, we'd be the first line of defense.

Pretty exciting stuff, though way more often than not, you sit on your bum twiddling your thumbs and otherwise trying to stay awake in a cramped cockpit with no temperature control. We were possibly on the brink of war with the PRC, but I was preparing myself to be mightily bored. In fact, I was praying for it. I did not want to fly and land in this dark.

On the flight deck, the wind moaned past us like the hungry ghosts of dead sailors on eternal quest for midrats. Dangle switched on a flashlight to prevent us from becoming casualties before we made it to our jets, as the pitching deck presented a grease-coated, slippery obstacle course of hazards.

All around, the invisible Pacific emitted an angry, hissing roar as the Boat zigzagged to keep any enemy out there guessing. Subdued floodlighting articulated the island stack, which housed the bridge and flight operations room.

Our jets rested at the catapult, ready to go. Wind gusted through the engine turbines to produce a metallic chitter. I walked over to mine and called up to Track and Siren. "Rise and shine, I'm coming up!"

Track descended the boarding ladder so we could switch places then followed me up.

"What are you reading now?" I asked him. Track was a history nerd who always had his nose in a book, and manning the Alert 7 offered prime reading time on his Kindle.

"Still working through Rick Atkinson's WW2 trilogy. It's pretty awesome."

"Cool." I plugged into the oxygen supply and adjusted my lap belts for a good fit while he updated me on the status of the aircraft, finishing with an explosive yawn.

"And with that, I'm gonna hit the rack," he said.

"When you get to the room, be really quiet, okay?"

"Why?"

"I don't want you to wake up your mom."

He laughed. "Shut up, Beaver."

The handoff complete, I chuckled and closed the canopy, which immediately misted with condensation. I'd been an aviator long enough that my cockpit checks were now second nature: external power connected, navigation system aligned, ready to go in seven.

This done, I slumped in my seat. "How are you, Guns?"

"Sick of stupid guys."

Snoop's all right," I said. "He just doesn't know any better."

"You know how hard it is?"

"What, being Taiwanese-American?"

"No, stupid. Being a woman in this squadron."

I honestly had no idea. "Is it bad?"

"Grow a pair of boobs, and then we can talk," Kyra said. "The fact my grandparents were born in China is just brown icing on the shit cake."

"When did they come to America?"

"They left after the civil war. They were Kuomintang. You could say I was born to hate the Communists. If we fight the PRC, it'll be very personal for me."

"Sorry, Guns. I didn't know any of this."

We'd spent a lot of hours shooting the bull in the jet, but I realized I'd been the one doing most of the talking, blathering about my big dreams and crappy childhood and which of my bunkmates was currently the most annoying.

She clicked on a red flashlight and cracked open a magazine. "It doesn't matter. After this deployment, my time's up, and I'm getting out."

"Jeez." I didn't know that either. The girl loved the rush of a challenge, but even carrier aviation wasn't enough for her—that, or it wasn't worth all the hassle anymore. "What are you gonna do when you're out?"

"I have a degree in cyber operations, so I guess I'll do something with that. Find a defense contractor and get paid big bucks to help guys like you fight the wars of the future."

Whatever she set out to do, I'm sure she'd do it. A part of me hoped she wouldn't walk away. A lot of aviators on the Boat talked about getting out and what they'd do, but many inevitably signed up for another few years.

I believed her, though. "You know, I'll really miss you, Guns."

"Aww, that's sweet."

We were truly alone, possibly for the first time. Between the darkness and condensation trickling down the canopy, I could barely see my plane captain. The flight deck heaved, reminding me we were perched on a platform floating in the middle of a vast and tempestuous ocean.

I know we were in a glass bubble that smelled like Track's armpits, doing a job that might require us to be flung roaring into utter darkness on a wet night, and sitting such that I'd have to contort my spine just to glimpse her face, but yeah, for me, it was somewhat romantic.

"We've spent a lot of time together," I said.

"We have," she agreed.

I'd rehearsed this moment many times in my fantasies. All the bold speeches and proposals bled away now that they approached reality. There was no better time for me to tell her my feelings, though. There might not be another time ever.

"I'm crazy about you," I blurted with all the grace of a depressurization fart.

"I'm sorry, what? What are you saying?"

"You're beautiful," I pressed on. "And smart and fierce, and a great WSO, and you don't take shit from anybody. I'd be proud to be with a lady like you."

Her flashlight clicked off. "I'm just not sure what you're asking."

"Well, what do you think of what I said?" Too scared to ask outright if she liked me back the way I liked her.

Kyra went quiet for a bit. "You try a little too hard to impress the other guys, and that makes me nervous. I don't know if you're you or somebody you're trying to be." Before I could respond, she added, "But you've shown me you have a good heart when it counts. I trust you."

I'd take that. "So." So, what? Honestly, I hadn't thought this far ahead. Earning my call sign, I'd acted on impulse and was now on dangerous ground.

"So the only dating the Navy allows on its boats is professional, platonic, and at least one foot apart," she pointed out.

"Right." My heart sank.

"And I'm getting out soon."

"Yeah." I was dying.

"So look me up after deployment, and we'll see what happens."

I smiled with joy and relief. "Did you just ask me out on a date?"

"Pick me up in San Francisco."

"I will definitely do that." I was already half-planning, half-imagining scenarios involving the best restaurant in town, champagne, dancing in moonlight.

"So how did this all happen?" she asked me. "When did you know?"

My face turned hot. "If I'm honest, do you promise not to think I'm a jerk?"

"That's a pretty loaded—"

"When I saw you in your room in your jammies, with your hair down. I thought you were smoking hot."

To my surprise, Kyra burst into laughter in the backseat.

"It wasn't until I got to know you that I started to

like-like you," I blustered. "So what about you? If you like me back, when did *you* know?"

"When you apologized to the chief," she said. "That impressed me. It took some character. You also handled the TOPGUN prank with more grace than most. That was the real you."

It's funny how the little incidents that scar you can add up to a big reward.

I said, "You telling me to talk to the chief was the first good advice I'd gotten since coming on the Boat—"

"Hang on a sec, Jack. Look outside."

There was a nervous energy among the deck crew, like somebody knew something.

"THIS IS THE TAO," the flight deck loudspeakers blared. It was the tactical action officer speaking. "NOW LAUNCH THE ALERT 7 FIGHTERS, INITIAL VECTOR TWO-FOUR-ZERO, CHECK IN WITH STRIKE BUTTON THREE. I SAY AGAIN—"

"Holy shit," I said. Something big was happening.

The radio buzzed in my ears. "We're go," Dangle said. "See you in the air."

I should have been scared by the prospect of flying into WW3 in bad weather on a pitch black night, but I was grinning like a fool as everything Kyra said finally sank in and I thought, *She likes me back!*

Within a few minutes, Dangle's Super Hornet roared down the track and zoomed off the carrier straight into the night. Colored wands waved again in the dark, beckoning me to taxi until I'd taken Dangle's place at the catapult.

The big metal blast deflector went up again. I ramped the engines to full power. Then it was our turn to fly, and the catapult cracked as it hurled us forward.

The deck edge lights blurred toward me in several breathless seconds, and then we thumped off the deck with the usual level of violence not unlike whiplashing straight through a brick wall.

The world around us became an endless black void, and suddenly I was flying on instruments alone, right hand working direction with the stick, left hand controlling speed with the throttles.

"Nightwing Three-Oh-Nine is airborne," I reported in, fighting vertigo.

Then I opened the throttles to catch up to my flight lead. At about ten miles out from the carrier, we rapidly climbed into the goo, where water molecules pelted the canopy and set our jet on a rocky road.

On the radio, Mother's controller was already handing Dangle off to an E-2 Hawkeye, a turboprop airborne early warning plane humming somewhere to the north. In the backseat, Kyra switched our UHF radio from the Departure frequency to Strike, which was being monitored by the westernmost cruiser in the carrier screen, battle watch captain reporting to the strike group's admiral, and Kyra's unpleasant roommate Medusa on the E-2, whose call sign was Olympus.

As air intercept controller, she'd vector us toward the unidentified flying object.

Dangle radioed me again on the squadron's common frequency. "Beaver, you got me?"

With the low cloud cover blocking the moon and stars, my electronically enhanced night vision gave me almost nothing. "I'm popeye."

"Tie on."

Most radio chatter goes like this. The lingo may

sound weird, but it has a point. While you're in the air, you don't macho-roughhouse or philosophize about friendship or confess big secrets like in a movie. Talk is for survival. Clarity and brevity rules, requiring a common tongue like software, ones and zeroes.

Incidentally, the same goes for slang, our other lingua franca. In the air, *I'm sweating fuel* always means, *I'm running on fumes and I'm not happy about it but I'm hanging tough*, with little room for interpretation.

Kyra painted the soup with our radar until we achieved a buddy lock on his jet. Thus informed and eventually guided by his exhaust plume, I vectored into position about a half-mile off his wing.

"Nightwing Lead is visual," I said.

Now holding hands as best we could, we headed toward the bogey with a rapid rate of closure. My HUD and helmet-mounted display overlaid my direction, acceleration, and angle of my wings relative to the airflow, what we call the angle of attack.

"Nightwing, Olympus," Medusa said. "Bogey, two-eight zero for twenty miles, low, track east, hot." Bearing, range, altitude, and that the bogey traveled east and was approaching us.

She added the bogey was a non-squawker, transponder off. The only way to identify this UFO was to fly close. The aircraft was running fast, silent, and just above the sea, seemingly on some kind of stealth mission.

Whoever this guy was, he was some kind of daredevil hotshot to fly fast and low over the swells on a Stygian night toward an American carrier strike group bristling with high-tech weaponry ranging from antiair missiles to Phalanx automatic guns. I had no doubt we were heading outbound toward a Chinese aviator who was determined to test us, show off, and earn a story. Even for fighter pilots, PLAN aviators were a notoriously macho breed and prone to aggressive stunts to prove their mettle against the high-and-mighty Americans.

"Elevator cherubs nine," Dangle ordered.

We pushed our noses down and leveled out at nine hundred feet. My job was relatively direct, consisting primarily of staying on his wing while keeping a second eye peeled. This was the power dynamic between a lead and his wingman, which fundamentally involves the wingman doing what he's told to be useful and ideally not doing anything detrimental. Which was fine with me as, despite Rowdy shouting in his ear, Dangle was a solid, reliable lead.

"I'm tally," he said, reporting he had contact on the aircraft on his forward-looking infrared radar. He confirmed ID as a J-15 Flying Shark, a carrier-based fighter plane produced by the People's Republic of China.

The "bogey," or unidentified aircraft, was now officially a "bandit." Unfriendly, though not necessarily hostile. We'd execute a stern conversion by coming up behind his 3/9 line.

"Roger," I radioed back.

We banked onto the bogey's six, descending in an energy-sustaining turn. Every bit of my attention was now devoured by the task of staying welded to Dangle's wing so I didn't lose him in the black. Visibility had improved, but I was still largely flying on instruments. I reminded myself the sea was practically right under me and not to drift into a surprise water landing.

If the bandit knew we were here, he didn't show it, and on approach he hadn't acquired either one of us in a radar lock, which would have instantly transformed our encounter into a far more intense interception.

Dangle accelerated onto an eight o'clock position behind the bandit, keeping things relatively friendly, while I flew about a mile behind and a little below him with a visual on his exhaust. He was in my missile envelope—within acceptable parameters for me to shoot and kill.

By now, we were broadcasting automatic warnings to this aviator that he was approaching a United States Navy carrier strike group on routine maneuvers in international waters, and to turn his ass around. He was exercising his right to international airspace the same way we were in these waters, but that didn't mean we'd allow him to barnstorm our carrier.

Comrade Wang would have to go home and be quick about it.

Whether to recon or test or provoke us, the Chinese bandit had tried to sneak past our defenses, and he'd done well for himself, but the game was up. At this point, if he did anything crazy, he was a dead man.

The carrier strike group consisted of a dozen warships in three major screens surrounding *Independence.* At its farthest reaches, picket ships and airborne early warning planes maintained constant vigilance. Then came the outer screen of ships with antisubmarine and antiair capabilities at twelve to twenty-five miles from Mother, and finally the inner screen with an antiair warfare emphasis. Immediately ahead lay the *Malvern Hill*, a Ticonderoga-class AEGIS guided-missile cruiser.

Still broadcasting automatic warnings, Dangle edged closer to the bandit hoping to steer him off his flight path and into a turn back toward *Hunan*.

"He's squawking now," Olympus informed us. "Positive ID as Chinese J-15."

"Copy," Dangle said then radioed the battle watch captain. "He's not budging. I'm going to—no, wait, one. His flashlight's on. He's signaling me."

Being on the bandit's six, I couldn't see anything, though I wished I could. A Chinese pilot wanted to tell us something, and I was real curious.

"He's shining the flashlight at his hand," Dangle said. "I'm edging a little closer for a look. He's trying to tell me or show me something."

Again I waited.

Dangle said, "He—ah, okay."

"Report," the battle watch captain said.

"He's, uh, flipping me the bird."

Dead silence on the radio. I wondered if the battle watch captain was sharing this bit of intelligence and unfolding battlespace development with the admiral.

He returned fuming. "Is he changing course?"

"Negative," Dangle answered.

The bandit was about to penetrate the strike group's outer screen.

"Nightwing Flight, direct your wingman to lock and stand by. He is to continue dry. Understand?"

I was authorized to acquire a radar lock but not authorized to release weapons.

"Solid copy," Dangle said and repeated the battle watch captain's order to me, finishing by asking me to repeat it back, which I did.

"Weapons status is tight," I confirmed.

"Beaver, you are go to show him our middle finger."

"Roger," I managed. My body was now flooded with adrenaline.

"We're having fun now," Kyra said in the backseat.

"Uh-huh." My mouth had turned to cotton.

I boresighted the radar and locked the J-15. A diamond-shaped target zone appeared around the bandit on my HUD. I was ready to shove a missile up his intake with the press of a few buttons.

The bandit knew we had a lock, as he jinked, no surprise since it's not a pleasant feeling to fly with a very powerful gun aimed at the back of your head.

Then he seemed to remember his cool and straightened out. After a few seconds of this, the aviator made a long, lazy, sweeping righthand turn to the south, as if he had all the time in the world and it was his idea.

Dangle and I stayed on him until he'd completed his turn, continuing to escort the trespasser off our property.

Now on an eastward course, the bandit lit his cans and headed for home.

The press would never hear about it, and historians would never record it, but I was the first American fighter pilot to gain a radar lock on the enemy on the eve of the Taiwan War. I gained enough notoriety from it that everybody on the Boat overlooked the fact that I got waved off and boltered twice on our return. Dangle received his own notoriety for getting the middle finger, which the aviators joked was a *casus belli*, and there was talk of giving him a new call sign: *Bird.*

After the interception incident, Mother shifted

from advertising her presence to avoiding detection. *Hunan* hugged us as it tried to shadow our movements, resulting in interceptions becoming a common occurrence. We all waited for the inevitable midair collision or weapons release that might start a war.

Instead, despite cyberattacks and blockade and missile threats, Taiwan flipped its own bird at the PRC and declared itself an independent and sovereign nation.

Within hours, bombs began to fall across the island.

TEN

In war, people die. There's always a last man to die just before it ends, and there's always a first when it's barely begun.

The day Pop shot down the J-15, I was seven stories above the flight deck, which offered the best views on the carrier. Outside the windows, the sun glittered on a bejeweled sea and silhouetted our nearest prowling escorts.

This was Primary Flight Control, a big glass box where the Air Boss, assisted by the Mini Boss and their team of controllers, coordinated the cyclical launch and recovery of aircraft and tracked them in the air. We were at the top of *Independence*'s island, its nerve center that included Flight Deck Control, the Bridge, and the other rooms used to direct the vast apparatus of the ship.

On the steel flattop below, steam billowed as a jet launched. The catapult thudded hard enough to tingle my feet. The Super Hornet's cans flared as it raced away from the bow.

"Launch complete," the Mini Boss said.

"Very well," the Air Boss growled, one hairy hand gripping the back of the elevated leather throne where he sat when flight ops weren't going on. Commander Donato had once commanded his own squadron and was in line for promotion to the prized rank of captain. Under black, bushy eyebrows, the flight maestro's dark gaze offered the impression of hammers looking for a handy anvil.

As for me, I was making a big contribution to these important operations by sitting on my ass twiddling my thumbs. It was my turn to don clean khakis and serve as the tower flower, the squadron liaison during air operations. I was here in case something went seriously wrong and to otherwise to serve as the mute receptacle for the Air Boss's colorful commentary about VFA-95's landing skills.

And boy, was he in a foul mood, which had its own pucker factor for me, given he was the absolute ruler over all flight ops. *Independence* zigzagging under strict radio and radar silence, the carrier running a heavy flight schedule, and various flight deck mishaps all made for a varsity day. For most daylight hours, the carrier had planes in the air, rocketing hundreds of miles away to keep *Hunan* at bay and probe the Chinese noose tightening around Taiwan.

We weren't at war, no, not yet, but it was in the air, as if borne on the salty wind. Chinese rocket forces had pounded Taiwan for weeks with hundreds of ballistic missiles, while the People's Liberation Army Air Force, or PLAAF, staged airstrikes around the clock. Any boat that could float was gathering at Hudong Shipyard in Fujian and other assembly points on China's coast. The world was deep into April now, one of the two months during the year ideal for crossing the Taiwan Strait without high risk of heavy fog or gales.

As for we intrepid Americans watching from the bench, our main job was to avoid detection, flex our muscle, and wait for *Ronald Reagan* and *Theodore Roosevelt*, which now streamed toward us from Hawaii and Japan. In days, we'd combine into a powerful armada of nearly forty warships and some two hundred fixed-wing and rotary aircraft, a larger air force than most countries. Meanwhile, *Abraham Lincoln* steamed across the Indian Ocean toward the South China Sea, increasing the pressure on the PRC.

America had taken the extraordinary step of recognizing Taiwan as a sovereign nation. Japanese and Vietnamese military forces were on high alert. Journalists shocked the world with scenes of carnage. China targeted military installations, but bombs missed, creating instant swathes of destruction, death, and human misery across sprawling modern cities.

A very big clock ticked down to something major happening. We all felt it. That unreal feeling of history in the making, and the world being at a crossroads.

Meanwhile, the carrier's eternal routines went on.

"Secure the cat," the Air Boss announced to the flight deck crews over the 5MC. "Prepare to recover aircraft."

Right then, though, I wasn't thinking about history or even my jets. My thoughts were presently in a shall we say idle if cardinal direction.

Kyra reached behind her head to unfasten her bun and allow her long, lustrous hair to spill wild around her shoulders.

With a coy smile, she—

The Mini Boss threw me the stink-eye. "You with us, Lieutenant?"

I jumped to attention. "Yes, sir!"

He smirked. "Glad to hear it. VFA-95 is about to recover."

Next to him, the Air Boss squeezed a stress ball a few times before tossing it aside to reach for his coffee. "Let's get these birds back on the farm."

Please, I prayed. *Don't let anything go wrong.*

Eager beaver I may have been, but I knew better than to ask for trouble to come my way today. I held my breath as the first jet thumped on the deck on the room's PLAT screen. It was Athena, and she landed without a glitch. Magic and Smoke were next. I was about to high-five myself when the fourth missed the wire and roared away in a wash of fire and exhaust.

Even without catching the tail code on the jet's vertical stabilizer, I could tell it was Snoopy in the cockpit. In fact, I almost chuckled and said, "That's so Snoopy," but I didn't think the Air Boss would find it as amusing.

I flinched in the aftermath and shot an anxious glance at him. Donato appeared to be simmering but not boiling. So far, so good.

"Three out of four ain't bad," the Mini Boss said, egging him on.

The Air Boss threw a glare in my direction. "What do you think, Beaver? Is three out of four *not bad*?"

"Well, to be honest, sir, I think it's whatever you say it is," I replied dutifully.

"Attaboy." He picked up his stress ball and crushed it in his fist.

Another landing flubbed for ol' Snoop, who appeared destined for another yellow button on the greenie board.

The Air Boss wasn't done with me. "When there's a bad status board, the captain has a bad day. When he has a bad day, I have a bad day. When I have a bad day—do you see where this is going, son?"

"Yes, sir."

"Is it clear in which direction gravity delivers the

turd avalanche?"

"I am reading you five by five, sir."

I wilted under the threat of those smoldering hammers, but he'd already turned away from me to bark orders at his team, as if even torturing me was boring. Still in a cold sweat, I gaped at the flight deck while I counted on my fingers.

One, two, three, four. Three landed, one boltered.

Leaning toward Commander Howard, I hissed, "I'm missing *two planes*, sir."

The Air Operations officer was listening intently to the voice at the other end of his headphones. With a scowl, he pointed at the status board. Though he didn't say a word, his finger seemed to yell *dumbass* at me.

I checked it over. Two jets had been tasked by the airborne E2 Hawkeye for an interception and would recover after. Pop led the section with Dangle and Rowdy riding his wing.

All of which meant I had to stick around. Another opportunity to excel, but I could relax. Everything was fine, perfectly fine.

"Oh, my God," Air Ops said in horror.

When I think of things I'd like to hear a veteran officer of numerous flight ops gasp in a carrier control room, *oh my God* would be near the bottom of the list.

Pretending to find the now-vacant PLAT fascinating, I leaned toward him in the hopes of eavesdropping on his conversation.

He turned in my direction, and I found myself jerking to startled attention again.

"You need to know there's been a, uh, incident," he said. "One of your birds went down. The wingman. Apparently, a midair with a Chinese hotdog. The flight lead's in a furball with the other Shark."

"Oh, my God," I said, which had been cued by a senior officer as an appropriate response, though what I wanted to do was scream, *Holy freaking shit!*

Dangle and Rowdy had gone down. And Pop was now fighting for his life.

Composing myself, I picked up the phone and dialed my squadron's ready room. Kyra was duty officer.

"Ready Room Three, Lieutenant Kyra Kao speaking."

"Hey, it's me." I made an effort to sound calm. "Is Tiger there?"

"Wait, one." I could tell she wanted to ask me what was wrong. I never could fool her.

"Tiger here," the skipper came on the line.

"Sir, this is Beaver in Pri-Fly. There's been an incident." I filled him in on everything I had, which wasn't much.

"Shit." He hung up so he could make his own calls.

I chafed and fidgeted as more information arrived in dribs and drabs. Some good news: "The flight lead shot down his Shark. Both Chinese aviators are KIA." And the worst: "The lead marked posit on his wingman, but nobody punched out." And then: "The lead is RTB, as he's at ladder state."

My brain automatically translated everything he'd told me into plain English while it spooled up to process it as reality. With Pop as flight lead, two Super Hornets had intercepted a pair of Chinese J-15 fighters. The aggressive PLAN aviators had played chicken with flybys past the nose, and the lead scraped his wingman off straight onto Pop's wingman, pulverizing both jets. Nobody ejected.

KIA means, "killed in action."

In the aftermath, Pop found himself in tight proximity to the other J-15, both of them wondering what the hell had just happened. I pictured both jets spiraling toward the sea, angling to get on the other's six, still unsure what to do. It ended with Pop knocking the Flying Shark out of the sky, marking the position, and heading home as he was running low on fuel.

I tried to relay all this to Tiger with more calls, but he was wired into the situation directly now, giving me little to do except stay informed.

Commander Howard flopped into his chair and rubbed his face with both hands. "Wait and see. This is a disaster. Shit's gonna hit the fan now."

I barely heard him. I'd flown with Dangle and Rowdy plenty of times. Dangle slept in the top rack across from me in my stateroom; Rowdy bunked with Kyra, so I'd seen her plenty of times during my visits. Now they were gone, very likely forever, and their absence formed a crushing weight on my chest.

No, I'm not going to pretend I'd lost my best friends. At times, Dangle had treated me like I was still FNG4, and Rowdy liked to call me out for making moony eyes at Kyra in the ready room, which was embarrassing.

Nonetheless, they were something like family. We were all connected on the Boat. I liked them fine, but I also loved them, and their loss was personal for me.

Kyra was going to take this even harder. I picked up the phone and called her.

The line connected, and she said, "Is it true?"

"I heard it from Air Ops, who heard it straight from the Hawkeye."

I could tell she was fighting hard to stay pro. "Nobody punched out?"

"Word is no survivors, but units are inbound to search the area."

"When are you off? I need you."

"As soon as Pop comes home."

"Come and find me when you're done up there, okay?"

"I will." Come hell or high water.

"Good."

"Hey, Kyra?"

"Yeah?"

"Sorry about Rowdy."

She let out a strangled whimper. "Thanks."

She hung up. Soon after, Snoopy flew in too high again but caught the last wire, not optimal but he'd made it, and yeah, he was alive.

"At least he landed on the right carrier," said the Air Boss, dry as dust.

He picked up his handset to blast Snoopy on the 5MC. My head snapped to fix him with a pointed stare.

On a normal day, this would earn me a starring role in a world of pain as Commander Donato's anvil, but he returned the handset and said, "Sorry about your people, Beaver."

"Thank you, sir." I slouched, suddenly exhausted.

"This is how wars start," Commander Howard muttered to himself, lost in thought. "Some hotdog shows off, and then it's World War Three."

"Fine," I said. At that moment, I was so mad I welcomed it.

He snapped out of his reverie. "I hope your boy makes it out of this."

"He's on his way back."

"I mean with his career intact. There'll probably be an investigation. We'll have to see what the tapes show."

When initiating combat, we were supposed to record the action.

"Jesus God," I swore in disgust. Not only had we lost two of our own, our strongest fighter might end up facing disciplinary action.

Pop landed forty-five minutes later, earning a rare smile from the Air Boss.

"This one could write the book," Commander Donato said.

"The man has style," agreed the Mini Boss. "Even after a furball."

"If he fights like he lands, that PRC stick didn't stand a chance."

Our Achilles was now safely aboard. Relieved, I raced breathless down the island's ladderwells to the ready room, now crowded with aviators.

No sign of Kyra or the Valkyries. Unsure what to do, I elbowed a path to Duke and Track.

My urgency had been for nothing. Once I reached them, I had no idea what to say. They stared back at me, looking as glum as I felt.

Around me, the squadron stirred. I turned to see Pop enter the room. The skipper walked next to him, one hand on the back of the aviator's neck as if donating strength.

A few people clapped, but Pop's glowering and distant expression silenced them. Instead, we cleared a path while crowding around to give his shoulders a light pat.

We know, we wanted to say. *We got you. Whatever load you're carrying, we'll share it.*

They promptly left, heading to Tiger's stateroom for a private talk about the future. China would almost certainly blame America and demand Pop's head. America would either cave or double down, hard to predict. Pop's superiors would go to the mat for him, how hard depending on what the tapes showed.

I turned to Duke. "I…"

He patted me on the shoulder as he walked away. "Yeah, Beaver."

"I'm heading to the Dirty Shirt," Track offered. "If you want to come."

Returning to my stateroom to stare at Dangle's empty bunk and try to sleep was the last thing I wanted to do, so his offer sounded solid to me. But I had somewhere important I needed to be. "I'll have to catch up with you."

I hurried down the crowded passageway to the Nest. Catching my breath, I knocked.

"Yeah?" Athena called out in a tone that said, *This had better be important.*

"It's Beaver," I said. "Kyra asked me to stop by, but I can—"

Amazon opened the door. "Get in here."

I stepped inside feeling hopeful for a lift. I'd always considered their stateroom an oasis of sorts. Life on the Boat might get heavy and boring and dangerous and occasionally nonsensical, but here, the women cast it all aside. They dressed in cute jammies, read magazines, let their hair down, and otherwise put their hardened warrior personas in the closet for a while. For me, it was the nearest I could get to walking off the ship and being back in the real world.

Now the women fought tears in a funereal atmosphere. Kyra sat coiled at her desk like a heat-seeking ball of fury. Perched on her top rack, Medusa hugged her ribs as she stared at the floor. Weeping had turned Amazon's mascara into raccoon splotches. Athena rubbed Siren's back to comfort her.

Remember, before, what I said about sympathy being rare in the Navy? It's true it's hard to find a sympathetic ear for one's typical bullshit. But when the chips are down, people in the service tend to close ranks and give each other whatever they need.

Today was one of those days.

"Hey," I said lamely. I was no good at this kind of thing. "I just wanted to say I'm sorry. Rowdy was…" What should I say? She was a good WSO? She sometimes made me laugh? "She was a good person."

The women nodded at this simple fact. Rowdy could be annoying and liked to embarrass me and sometimes ate with her mouth open, but she *was* a good person. Now that she was dead, it became natural to see only the good.

Kyra stood. "Thanks for coming, Jack."

"Are you okay—"

She crossed the room, cupped my surprised face in her hands, and pulled me in for a chaste but loving kiss. My senses reeled, barely registering the Valkyries' gasps of surprise, instead keenly aware of her body in proximity to mine.

She pulled back, her dark eyes glittering up at my stunned, stupid expression, and I was about to suggest we find an unoccupied ventilation room when a tiny voice of reason informed me the kiss had been about comfort, not sex, and need, not want.

"I'm sorry," I said and held her against me in a warm hug.

I hoped she found it as comforting as I did.

ELEVEN

Allegedly of Chinese origin, a curse goes: "May you live in interesting times."

Out in the Philippine Sea, things were about to get very interesting.

Most mornings, you wake up, and the day passes in banal routine. Others, you get dressed, comb your hair, grab some breakfast, and then boom, something big happens that changes the world.

My big something was coming fast.

When it started, I was enthroned in the head with my flight suit balled around my ankles. *Independence* boasted the latest in high-tech, vacuum-powered shitters, which nonetheless often clogged and required a colossally expensive acid flush to clean out, billed to the taxpayer.

And here was your intrepid narrator, putting the system to the test. Though I was on alert status and had to make it quick, I was enjoying the rare few minutes of quiet and solitude—

"THIS IS THE TAO," the 1MC blared. "NOW LAUNCH THE ALERT 7 FIGHTERS—"

I jumped as if electrocuted but then relaxed. I was on Alert 15, not 7, status.

The 1MC blatted: "LAUNCH THE ALERT 15! I SAY AGAIN, LAUNCH—"

"Damn it!" I pulled up my flight suit and floundered into the passageway trailing toilet paper. "Gangway! I'm on alert!"

Sailors dodged as I raced to my ready room.

Kyra eyed my flushed face. "You run a marathon or something?"

I hurried past her exuding a black cloud of frustration. *This had better be good*, I thought at the time. The heavy flying schedule over the past few weeks had battered my body and drained me to irritable exhaustion. The constant harassment and showing off by the Chinese pilots, which culminated in two of our aviators dying, had pissed us all right off. The only daily ritual that offered a moment's peace and quiet had been abruptly interrupted.

So yeah, this had better be big. It'd better be the start of Armageddon.

Careful what you wish for, right?

We didn't know it at the time, but we were about to get served Armageddon with a side of Ragnarök.

In the paraloft, we found Pop shrugging on his harness. Last night, the guy watched his wingman fall out of the sky in pieces, shot down an enemy plane in a tense, close-quarters dogfight, and flew back to find out he faced an investigation.

Now he was flying right back into it, a reminder that while all this may have often felt like a movie, in the real world your story doesn't end after you survive and win your big, bloody fight. You wake up the next morning, drink your coffee, and get back to business.

I stepped into my G-suit. "What's the word, Pop?"

"Bandits approaching the foul line."

Kyra put on her helmet. "Why do they need the Alert 15 for that?"

"A *lot* of bandits. The Hawkeye will brief us in the air. Let's go."

I exchanged a wide-eyed glance with Kyra. A big

show of force might just mean a shooting war, either the intentional or the accidental kind.

After news of last night's incident raced up the chain of command to Hawaii and then Washington, the scuttlebutt had it an admiral got woken up by the news and then make a tense phone call to his counterpart in Beijing.

After the obligatory shouting and finger pointing concluded, the admiral declared a longitudinal foul line across which America would not cross, and which America would consider Chinese forces hostile if they crossed. Early this morning, the entire squadron had been yanked out of their racks to receive the new rules of engagement, or ROE, which were simple. If PLAN fighters crossed the line with clearly hostile intent, we were authorized to shoot.

This pleased us for reasons that should be obvious. Topping the list was the existing ROE didn't allow us to shoot unless we were shot at, and it's kind of hard to shoot while you're getting sucker punched by and running howling from air-to-air missiles. Besides that, the foul line would solve the problem of our having to constantly intercept Chinese fighters flown by aviators with big chips on their shoulders, a problem that would only grow worse when *Theodore Roosevelt* arrived in two days and *Ronald Reagan* the day after that.

The solution wasn't perfect, though. Not by a long shot. *Clearly hostile intent* remained open to interpretation. The foul line was also unilaterally recognized, namely just by us; China, which considered the East China Sea its bathtub and us irritating and unwelcome "guests" who wouldn't go home, had agreed to us staying on our side but not necessarily to their own ships and aviators doing the same.

Pop frowned at us. "Listen, we might be flying into something new today. New for all of us. It's going to take some courage."

I put on my game face. "They don't scare us, do they, Guns?"

"You're brave," he said.

I set my mouth in a grim, battle-hardened smile. "Well, Pop, I—"

"Bravery is stupid. Everybody gets scared. What you need is courage. Courage is you're scared but you do it anyway. You lean into it. You get aggressive. And most important? You keep your cool. When in doubt, remember your training."

"Copy that, Pop," Kyra said, her dark eyes wide as saucers.

As for me, I was in heaven; this was exactly the kind of warrior heart to heart I'd dreamed of having ever since I boarded the Boat. If this *were* a movie, I'd relate how he told us to believe in ourselves and fight for our country like true American heroes. He didn't. Not because they were dumb platitudes, but because we took these things for granted.

Instead, he told us to stay focused with absolute discipline on the mission, ROE, safety, and all that we'd learned. The fact he was eating up precious seconds saying this spoke volumes about its importance.

"Now let's go answer the door and see what Comrade Wang wants." He headed out to the catwalk leading to the flight deck ladderwell.

This was as inspiring as things got, but he'd inspired us just the same. Setting our jaws in twin professional scowls, Kyra and I followed.

Loaded with fifty pounds of gear from thigh boards to helmet, we dashed as fast as we could to our grease-splattered, preflighted jet and mounted it. In the cockpit, I situated my charts and bags, connected the air hose, and buckled up.

The canopy slid down the rail and locked.

"I think you need a new call sign," Kyra said as she ran her instrument checks. "Because the one you got isn't working."

I blinked in surprise. "What do you mean?"

"I kissed you last night, and you haven't said boo about it."

"You want to talk about this *now*?" Sam had started to walk me through the startup sequence. The number two engine growled into action.

"I'm wondering why you didn't suggest taking it further, that's all."

The handiest answer was it would land us in a heap of trouble, but that wasn't the whole truth. "You were upset. I didn't want to, you know, take advantage. I like you, Kyra."

"An officer *and* a gentleman," she mused. "I hadn't guessed."

"It says so right on my commission." It actually did. When I was commissioned, I became an Officer and a Gentleman as authorized by an Act of Congress.

She laughed as the number one engine roared to life. "Okay, Mr. Gentleman, let's go and show Comrade who's boss."

An airman waved us forward to take tension at the bow catapult. The massive steel blast deflector raised behind us. I throttled to full power, wiped out the flight controls, and waited for the final flurry of thumbs-up from the airmen.

Kyra said, "We're still on for San Fran after deployment, though, right?"

"What?" I saluted the crew, signaling we were ready to launch. "Oh God, yes."

"Good. Because you know what I think we might end up doing?"

Then she told me.

The jet exploded down the track, propelled by seventeen tons of thrust.

Seconds later, we hurtled off the deck like a cannon shot and vaulted into empty space. My brain reeling from G forces and desire, I grabbed the stick and tipped my wing to bank west onto Pop's track.

Ahead, my flight lead was a tiny black dot disappearing into the late afternoon sun. I took off after him. The rendezvous point was a hundred miles away, where we'd be out of the EMCON Alpha area and allowed to use radios and radar.

"Recommend gate," Kyra said. Putting the pedal to the metal by lighting the blowers.

We had to get to the rendezvous point quickly, but I didn't want to unnecessarily burn fuel, which we might need later. "I'll bump it up a bit."

Trailing twin trails of morning water vapor from the wings, the jet hurtled after Pop's and began to overtake it. From what he'd said, this promised to be an important party, and we were already late to it.

I caught up to him and throttled down to canter on his left wing. At a distance of ten miles from Mother, we climbed through a big patch of cottony cumulus and rapidly gained an altitude of twenty thousand feet. Aided by fairly clear skies above the middle cumulus layer, we raced through the atmosphere over a landscape of bright, billowing white.

Departure was silent as *Independence* was still at EMCON Alpha, so Kyra tuned into the Strike frequency monitored by the Hawkeye, battle watch captain, and the USS *Trenton*, the nearest ship in Mother's screen.

The air intercept controller vectored us into a rendezvous with the Alert 7 and the CAP now plowing an oval in the sky. It was my old pal Medusa, with her annoyed glare every time I invaded her stateroom to see her roommate. With our arrival, the strike group organized for the interception.

Like a ballet, we broke into formation and sounded off over the radio: me and Kyra, Pop, Tiger, Nine Lives, Athena, Track, Pepsi Man and Siren, and Sparky and Duke, with Playboy piloting a trailing Growler, basically a modified two-seat F/A-18 that specialized in electronic warfare.

I stayed glued to Pop's left wing, my head jerking between my twelve, my lead, and my six. The clouds parted to offer a view of the *Trenton* far below. From up here, the guided-missile cruiser looked like a child's bathtub toy, visible mostly by its foamy track.

"Nightwing, Olympus," Medusa radioed. "Single group, ID PLAN J-15s, bearing two-seven-five from Nightwing for one-five-zero miles, angels high, track east, hot. Recommend commit."

"Nightwing commits," Tiger replied. On the squadron common frequency on the secondary radio, he ordered us Gargoyles, "Check tapes, arm hot."

Mouth dry, I flipped the weapons console's Master Arm switch to ARM.

My Super Hornet was now fangs out, ready to radiate destruction.

This plane carries eleven weapons hardpoints. My wingtips bristled with heatseeking Sidewinder missiles. Under the wings and fuselage, I carried AIM-120 AMRAAMs, big and beautiful missiles equipped with active radar guidance.

Due to their standoff range and tracking, you can fire an AIM-120 over the horizon and destroy a target long before you see it. Instead of guiding the missile to the target, you can fire and forget.

Besides missiles, I also had a Vulcan rotary cannon mounted on my jet's pointy end, ready to spray more than four hundred 20-millimeter rounds.

Facing us head on in a rapid rate of closure were J-15 Flying Sharks. The superior offspring of the Soviet-designed Su-27 Flanker, this multirole fighter flies a little faster than the Super Hornet and is able to reach higher altitudes and handle stronger G forces, which enables harder maneuvering.

The plane suffers its own weaknesses, though. Most notable was these particular bandits had almost certainly taken off from *Hunan*, an older carrier based on a Soviet design. As a result, they could only get into the air carrying around three thousand pounds of weapons compared to eighteen thousand for our Rhinos, and the PLAN's midair refueling capability was relatively weak.

I reminded myself the biggest asset I had was me. Not because I was particularly awesome, as I wasn't, but because I was a United States Navy aviator, recipient of a colossal amount of advanced training and practice and led by capable officers with deep experience.

While I was still pretty green relative to the senior Gargoyles, I was far better trained than the average PLAN aviator.

I tried to take some comfort in this, but my helmet became hot and chafing.

Medusa returned to the radio. "Nightwing, Olympus shows pop-up second group. Lead group, bullseye, fifty-five miles." She'd called the bandits' range to the "bullseye," or our reference point, which was the longitude that constituted the foul line we were guarding. "Trail group, bearing two-eight-zero from Nightwing for two hundred miles. Angels twenty, hot."

Kyra whistled. I responded with a startled nod, though she couldn't see it. Either the Chinese were staging an excessive demonstration of force, or we were about to get clobbered.

Either way, we'd find out very soon.

"They're heading directly to Mother," she said, her voice wispy and breathless. "They know where she is."

I gulped. "Uh-huh."

Somehow, the Chinese had located our carrier. A lucky submarine? A satellite or high-altitude drone racing overhead? I didn't think about it. I was way more concerned that this was going to end in missile launch, and what that meant. If it didn't, if this were all an act on the part of the Chinese, they deserved an Oscar.

Back in the paraloft, I'd stuck out my chest and put on a brave front, but brave really was stupid. Fear of dying didn't bother me, at least not then. I actually thought I'd get through any combat without a scratch. If I didn't earnestly believe I was invincible, I wouldn't be in jets; it was part of the DNA of a fighter pilot.

Mostly, I was afraid I'd screw the pooch and mess up. That I was my biggest liability, not my best asset. That I wasn't ready for this and didn't have the chops for aerial combat and its split-second, life-and-death decision-making. That I was a screwup playing at being a fighter pilot, a faker who'd get my comrades killed. It was the same old disease that infects most rookies, the same that made guys like Snoopy more of an enemy to themselves than any bandit.

Cool as cucumber, Tiger corrected our heading to maintain the direct intercept. Reminded of my duty, the training kicked back in. After glancing at my HUD, I focused on Pop to make sure I stayed properly attached to his wing.

"Nightwing, request," the skipper said.

"Olympus, say request," Medusa shot back.

"Clarify ROE to designate any aircraft crossing the foul line and nose hot as hostile." The nose being the business end of the jet, a hot nose meaning it and its radar and weapons were aimed at you, a very provocative act by itself.

"Stand by, Nightwing."

The battle watch captain came onto Strike. "Nightwing Flight, give the bandits maximum leeway." I sensed every aviator in the formation flinching along with me; the situation did not call for nuance. The captain clarified, "If they pass the foul line and lock onto you, you are authorized to shoot. Otherwise, weapons tight."

"Roger," Tiger growled. Clear as mud, though I was somewhat relieved, as my CO's request would have had us shooting if the Chinese tested the foul line even a mile. "Committed." Confirming we were going ahead with the intercept as fragged. "Dope?"

"Olympus shows lead group, bullseye, forty-five miles," Medusa responded.

"We getting any more support?"

"Mother has four Rhinos on route, nine minutes out."

"Copy." Right now, that seemed like a *very* long time.

"And, uh, we ID'd the trail group as PLAAF H-6 bombers."

"We're about to be attacked," Kyra said in the backseat.

"Okay," I said. Sucking pure oxygen from my hose in rapid breaths, my voice sounded tinny and distant in my ears. I was close to what veteran aviators call a *helmet fire*, overstimulation in combat, and I wasn't even fighting yet.

Medusa returned to the radio. "Nightwing, Olympus, popup third group of bandits, two-eight-zero from Nightwing for one-three-zero miles, angels high, hot."

"Copy," the skipper said, now sounding annoyed. "Nightwing, target lead group. Olympus, monitor the trail groups."

We now faced three waves of bandits, the two fighter groups separated by fifty miles. The radio went quiet as the aviators steeled themselves for combat.

"We got this, Guns," I said, convincing nobody.

"Yeah," she said mechanically. "We do."

Our radar went on pulsing, painting the sky in front of us.

God, get us through this, I prayed, *and I'll...*

And I'll what?

We took it for granted God stood on our side, but

that didn't mean the Almighty had taken an interest in my personal survival.

I'll try to be good.

My displays lit up with potential targets as the radar bleated multiple air-to-air contacts. Voices crashed the radio as aviators called out theirs. The first wave of J-15s was within eighty miles now and rapidly approaching the foul line. I squirmed in a puddle of nervous sweat.

My bargaining done, I went straight to acceptance. I'd do my best for the comrades on my wings and the tough lady in my backseat. They depended on me to do my job, so I'd do it. *I* wasn't going to fight and win; I was going to get my head out of my own way so I could allow my training to fight and win.

My head jerked between my HUD and wings, and my hand worked the stick of its own accord as I allowed all that training to take over, all the endless hours of tough drilling and practice I'd done until flying had become nearly as second nature to me as jogging.

Lean into it. Get aggressive.

From acceptance, I discovered anger.

I was now ready to fight.

TWELVE

In war, whether you individually survive or die, triumph or lose, become a hero or don't, well, a lot of it comes down to dumb luck. All the training, all the planning, all the leadership, it's about getting better odds when you bet your life.

As I'd find out firsthand. My first big battle was about to begin.

Right now, though, we were still playing our long-range game of chicken, and neither side was flinching.

"Nightwing, roll tape," the skipper said. "Assume combat spread."

Dispersion in our flying formation widened for defensive advantage and shifted to line abreast, a moving wall of incredible firepower. I raised the elevators and climbed to about fifteen hundred feet above my flight lead.

Our Rhinos and the J-15s closed at a rate topping nine hundred knots.

Both sides were now in missile range.

The Chinese rapidly approached the foul line.

"Defensive!" Gargoyles yelled on the radio, while my console toned its own warning. I echoed that I was spiked as well.

Somewhere out there, a bandit had me radar-locked.

"Nightwing, tag a target," Tiger growled. "Turn on the music."

My console bonged as Kyra gained a lock on one of the approaching planes. The Growler trailing our formation activated radar jamming. From my STORES page, I selected AIM-120 AMRAAM.

Dead silence on the radio. The sky a radiant blue. The sun glaring in my eyes. Seconds grinding slowly past. Sweat trickling under my oxygen mask.

The HUD displayed my diamond-bracketed target's heading, airspeed, closure rate, and aspect angle, or angle between his nose and mine.

I wondered what the Chinese aviator was thinking and feeling right now.

I didn't have to wonder long. My shoulders clenched as my missile warning system detected the distinct thermal signature of launches.

"Missiles in the air!" somebody called out.

A *lot* of PL-12 missiles, the PRC's answer to the AMRAAM, now hurtling toward us at three thousand miles an hour.

I still couldn't even see the Chinese fighters. They'd fired at standoff range.

"Nightwing, cleared to kill," Tiger said. "Fox Three!"

I mashed my control stick's pickle switch. "Fox Three!"

My airframe thumped as three hundred pounds dropped from one of my wings. Twelve feet long, the AIM-120 streaked away at nearly Mach 4.

Trailing smoke, missiles reached out from our formation toward the horizon. I didn't see any coming back at us, as the PL-12 used smokeless rocket fuel. My console assured me they were there, and one was going to try to kill me. Dedicated, able to turn on a dime under extreme G forces, and nearly as fast as a bullet.

"Lost lock!" Kyra said.

The targets started to jump across my radar attack display. The Chinese had brought a Growler Shark with them, an electronic warfare plane equivalent to our Growler. Its "music" messed with our targeting system. We'd just lost our radar lock and missile tracking.

Not good.

I pitched my nose down and plunged into a high-energy dive at full throttles.

Of course, our Growler's electronic warfare system might have made the missile hunting me lose its tracking, but I wasn't sticking around to find out.

When an active radar missile is coming for you, you have three defenses. Outrun it, maneuver it abeam when it's about to hit, and dump chaff—a cloud of glass fibers covered in aluminum—in the hope it'll attack this decoy or it'll go stupid until its rocket motor burns out.

If none of that works, kiss your ass goodbye.

Assisted by gravity, my Super Hornet hurtled toward the deck so fast that negative-G sucked me up against my belts and flipped my stomach as if it were a flapjack. We dropped through the middle cloud layer, revealing additional thick tufts of cumulous below to my now-bulging eyes.

We burst through them. The glittering sea filled my windshield. Nothing down there that might distract a homing missile.

"Altitude," Bitching Betty scolded in her Tennessee twang, sounding again just like my mother. "Altitude." The alarm whooped.

I pulled back on my stick with my nose pointed

toward where I believed the missile was coming from, hoping we could get something on radar. Sucking me toward the roof, gravity now crashed down on me with the force of an avalanche. My G suit inflated around my waist and legs to keep the blood in my head.

Barely in control of my aircraft, I strained at the stick.

"Hick," I gasped, taking short, quick breaths that I'd been trained to do to avoid graying or blacking out from excessive G force. "Hick! Hick!"

Behind me, Kyra paused from her own hicking to howl, "It's still—*BREAK RIGHT!*"

I throttled back and snap rolled into a high-G turn to put the missile on my beam. My body weight rocketed to sevenfold as the Super Hornet pivoted ninety degrees. Kyra punched a cloud of aluminum confetti into our wake.

Once we pulled out, I craned my neck to try to see behind me. "Where is it?"

"We're good!" she gasped. "It went stupid."

"Okay!" I yelled and swore, "Jesus, God!"

Then I laughed, and she laughed with me. The laughter of the mad.

Now that the immediate threat had passed, I could stop boresighting and gain some situational awareness. Heavy breathing and excited chatter filled the radio. *Two, bandit, right, four!* Then: *Splash one!*, letting us all know somebody had scored a kill. Our radar blinked contacts before it spewed garbage again and blanked. *Splash two!* I ignored it to eyeball the sky.

In their escape from the missiles, it seemed everybody had dived into the weeds and now jockeyed for altitude and position. I spotted a Super Hornet climbing north after shooting down a J-15, with two more veering after him in pursuit.

It was Pop.

I rose into a steep and rapid climb. "I hope you're checking our six."

"Duh," Kyra responded. "We're clean."

I rolled inverted to check underneath us and then righted again, jettisoning my empty drop fuel tanks to eliminate some dead weight for the fight.

"Okay," I breathed. "We're in business."

Time for a little loose deuce and freelance mayhem.

I radioed Pop. "Tally two bandits on your tail. I'm on the way."

"Copy, Beaver," he acknowledged. "I'll keep them busy."

Pop leveled out his climb and tried to turn defensively into the approaching bandits so we could bracket them, but they were too fast and had the drop on him.

He veered away and floored it. While he hadn't been able to turn in time, the good news was his pursuers were focused only on him, priming me for a swing.

"Smoke is defending!"

"Fox Two!"

"Mayday, Nine Lives is hit! I see a chute!"

"Splash three!"

I veered into position below and behind the bandits' 3/9. My speed and aspect angle were a little high, which risked overshooting and inadvertently exiting the fight if things suddenly changed—as they usually did—but I decided to risk it.

My joint helmet-mounted cueing system gave me an advantage here, as I could aim and shoot my Sidewinders off boresight, or at angles up to around eighty degrees off the nose, using my helmet display. But first I had to get close enough for the shot.

The trailing fighter entered my missile envelope. I selected a Sidewinder and waited for the tone telling me it had found a hot spot for homing.

I snarled. "Got you, mother—"

The Flying Sharks banked right in unison, and I rolled with them into a hard turn while throttling back and applying the speed brakes.

Dogfighting is all about aspect, where your nose is in relation to your foe's. You are constantly negotiating altitude and airspeed for nose position and then recovering to replenish energy if you bleed too much of it.

When I came out of the turn, I'd lost the range.

"Damn it." I pictured them laughing, though I didn't think they'd seen me. I aimed the nose down in an energy-sustaining turn and worked to regain my position on the bandits' six.

"Use Pop!" Kyra advised. "*They're* chasing *him*."

"Anytime, Beaver," Pop said.

Dogfighting is fluid, as much art as skill. You don't fight in the present. You fight in the future. You try to predict your opponent's every move and fly according to where he'll go next.

I switched my pursuit from the bandits—who still didn't know a capitalist running dog was stalking them—to Pop, visually the size of a gnat against the sky. My Rhino scraped the atmosphere in a lagging pursuit of the Chinese wingman.

Second by second, I gained ground behind his 3/9 line. I was boresighting now, trusting Kyra to keep her eyes peeled for a sucker punch.

The PLAN flight lead fired a missile, which shot off into the blue.

"Missile in the air, Pop," I cried into the radio. "Break left, throttles!"

He banked, dumping an arc of flares. The Chinese aviators used the time to improve their position for a possible gun attack. I came out of my own turn and waited for the wingman to enter my kill zone.

The console emitted a loud buzz as the Sidewinder searched for its hot spot. The buzz's pitch escalated to a piercing cat's growl as it locked.

"Fucking A," Kyra said. Suddenly, it was Christmas.

I squeezed the trigger. "Fox Two!"

The Sidewinder whooshed off the rail toward the trailing fighter. We were flying away from the sun now, and the only clouds were below us, an ideal setup for heat homing.

Blinded to my attack from below, his eyes welded to his leader and prey, the wingman was caught flat-footed. He broke out of formation as the heat seeker curled toward his tailpipe and exploded, shredding his tail in a cloud of smoke and flying metal. The engine flashed a big fireball and began trailing black smoke.

The pilot ejected as the shattered jet spiraled to disappear in the clouds below.

"Splash four!" I whooped and pumped my fist.

And promptly overshot as the lead continued his left turn. I spared a glance at Pop, who'd twisted away from the heat seeker. I didn't have enough energy for another break, so I swung into a wide, descending turn, arcing away from the combatants. I radioed Pop my position and suggested a simple plan.

"Splash five!" Athena crowed on the radio.

After a few seconds of mental calculations, Pop agreed. "Be there."

"Roger," I said and called to the backseat, "Hang on to your hat—"

"Hostile," Kyra yelled back. "Right, two o'clock high!"

The Flying Shark bore down on me at an oblique angle like a monstrous bird of prey.

His racks empty, he opened up with his cannon.

I jinked on reflex, my Rhino bobbing as thirty-millimeter rounds slashed the air and tracers flashed past like laser blasts. The J-15 seemed to grow larger by the second, the big gun winking on the nose, slowly correcting its devastating fire.

I grabbed an AIM-120. "Fox Three!"

The AIM-120 whooshed away. A moment later, my jet shook violently as smoking holes appeared in the wing.

The missile detonated in front of the cockpit in a terrific airburst. The J-15's nose disappeared. The rest of it pitched forward into an incredible somersault that hurtled straight at me.

I froze, mesmerized and caught completely flat-footed. Jinking wasn't going to cut it. I was in a turn and wouldn't be able to evade in time.

The only thing that saved me was pure, dumb luck.

The wreck cartwheeled right over my bubble, blotting out all light for a moment as it vaulted past with a virtually indescribable sound, something like a cross between a passing freight train and the world's biggest piece of cardboard ripping down the middle. One of the wings broke off to tumble away into the ether.

Then it was gone, though even then the enemy pilot tried to take me into the drink with him as trailing debris battered my airframe. A chunk of metal the size of a baseball cracked against the Plexiglas, but that didn't worry me. What did was the strong possibility of just one little screw or nut getting sucked into my engines.

Luck saved me yet again. I shook my head as we continued our wide turn, unable to believe that just happened.

"Splash six," I croaked.

"Jesus, God," Kyra finally managed.

This time, we didn't laugh.

"On the way, Pop," I radioed. "I'm hit but flyable."

"Push hard if able," he urged. "My panel's red."

The heat seeker had missed him, but he'd taken some critical damage from it. Warning indicators were lighting up on his dashboard.

I was about to exit my turn. Trailing a long, thin stream of white smoke, Pop struggled across the sky while the bandit gained aspect on him and readied for a gun shot.

What the bandit didn't know was Pop was dragging him across my line of fire. Which was brilliant on our part, if I could get there on time. He was jinking like crazy to delay the inevitable, but I didn't think Pop's Rhino had the strength for more hard maneuvers.

After bleeding off so much energy and with the damage to my wing increasing drag, I'm not sure how much stamina mine had either. My stick had gone gluey. I kept the heel of my hand pushed against the throttles for more thrust, but I felt like I was standing still, a very unsettling feeling when there are planes all around you shooting at each other. In combat, speed is what keeps you alive.

The Chinese pilot saw me coming, sized up his overall odds at gaining a kill versus getting out of this alive, and promptly banked away from the fight into a steep dive.

"The bandit on your tail bugged out, Pop," I said in wonder.

"That works for me. Rejoin."

The other Gargoyles reported that their quarry were egressing to the west. Both of the Chinese jets had been damaged and were limping. The Americans pursued them to the foul line before turning back.

"Nightwing, Sierra Hotel," Tiger congratulated us, giving us all the ultimate attaboy: *shit hot*. "Terminate and rejoin, then stand by for roll call." He added on the primary, "Hawkeye from Nightwing, ETA on the gorilla?"

"Trail groups are withdrawing," a very tense Medusa answered. "No inbound red activity on radar."

Before we could sigh with relief, the battle watch captain cut in. "Nightwing Flight, be advised the bombers launched vampires." Antiship cruise missiles. "The *Trenton* was hit."

A long pause. "Copy."

"What luck?" Asking how we were doing.

"Mission success. Wait one for report." There was plenty to unpack, but Tiger needed to evaluate his assets. "Nightwing, roll call, and say state."

Two planes had gone down. Nine Lives had ejected and floated somewhere on the sea. Track had not. The skipper called in positions for search and rescue. Pop reported that his and my Rhinos had taken damage but were flyable.

The battle watch captain had a new tasking for the Gargoyles. Tiger rattled off orders. Pepsi Man and Athena would remain on station to support the rescue efforts. Tiger would lead a division to support the *Malvern Hill* as it engaged in rescue operations at the dying *Trenton*. A tanker would meet them there for midair refueling. The four Super Hornets still on route from *Independence* would relieve them soon.

As the Navy was now at war and flew in hostile territory, the skipper advised all of us to stick to the established recovery routes to avoid receiving blue on blue fire from jittery American warships.

Pop's Rhino and my own jet were flyable but had sustained damage, so we were fragged to RTB. We were out of the big game.

Being Beaver, I naturally chafed at this news, but Pop's Rhino flew with a gut shot that had disabled the right engine, my damaged wing whistled with worrying vibrations, and with the sun setting, we'd have to find our own tanker, refuel, and then land in the dark.

In short, our simple RTB promised plenty of pucker factor.

"Wow," I said as I returned my cockpit switches to where they were before the fighting started.

"Yeah," Kyra deadpanned. "Wow."

I wanted to talk about the battle, but I didn't even know where to begin. "I thought that Shark was gonna run right smack into us."

"We can talk when my boots are back on the deck." She sounded drained.

"Sorry."

"It's okay. I'm just trying to process what happened. I don't know whether to pass out from hypoxia or crawl out of my skin. I'm shaking from adrenaline."

I was feeling pretty chuffed about my warrior skills and had hoped for a dramatic replay of the fight—with me humbly downplaying my two kills and insisting Pop played a key role while Kyra argued that no, no, really, I *was* awesome—but no deal. What I *didn't* want to think about was the second empty bunk in my stateroom and the man who'd occupied it, or about the fact that I'd just taken the life of a human being before he could do the same to me.

"And if we're ever in a fight like that again, start with the AIM-120s and work them until you can't," Kyra added. "Then go to the Sidewinders."

"Well," I said, chastened. "We did good anyway."

"We were lucky. Now stop talking."

I replayed it all in my head and realized how right she was. I'd dodged a PL-12 that refused to be dissuaded by remote jamming. Not a single PLAN shooter acquired a position behind my 3/9 the entire time. The wingman hadn't seen me coming even after I flew into an overshoot.

And more: The next pilot who'd fired his guns had dinged me but otherwise missed at fairly close range and also missed hitting my ordnance. My responding missile had traveled just enough distance to arm in time. The wreckage flew right over my gaping face. The last pilot decided to bug out instead of put in a little extra effort first that might have given him the chance to turn Pop into pink mist.

I looked over to inspect my wing. The charred and puckered holes whistled. The jet fought increased drag and was a little unbalanced, but it remained flyable.

When I added up all my breaks, it was enough to make me believe in guardian angels or that I maybe carried a horseshoe up my ass.

I didn't overlook the fact I was also lucky to have Kyra in the backseat.

"Lucky, yeah," I said. "But you did good, Guns. We make a good team—"

A flash lit up the thickening darkness outside.

Flames flickered around Pop's left engine.

"Heads up, Pop," I said into the radio. "Engine fire, left!"

"Mayday, mayday, mayday," he said. "Shutting down engine one."

Silence returned to the radio. I said, "The fire seems to be out."

Smoke clouds puffed from the engine to be carried away by his slipstream. I pictured him working through emergency procedures.

"Restart failed. I'm dead stick." He'd begun coasting in an altitude-losing glide. "Well, shit. I reckon that's it."

Eyes glued to his engine, I stayed quiet.

Pop sighed. "I'm punching out."

The idea of ejecting somewhere over nowhere in the Pacific at twilight filled me with terror, and I wasn't even the one doing the ejecting. Pop, however, coolly radioed the Hawkeye to tell Medusa the bad news.

She replied that combat search and rescue assets nearby were on route to pick up Nine Lives and would get to him right after, and she'd take command of the scene so I could RTB and assume radio silence for EMCON.

He rogered and said, "You get all that, Beaver?"

I fought to control my voice. "After you punch, we'll stick around to mark your posit and drift. We'll check in with you on the search and rescue frequency."

"Well," Pop said. He was quickly losing altitude. "This ought to be real interesting."

I flinched as his canopy flew away and he burst from the cockpit, a violent and terrifying process, not to mention dangerous.

The chute deployed, and he was on his way to the dark sea.

After Kyra called in his position, I tuned to the SAR frequency. "Pop! How copy?"

"I got you," Pop said over his handheld radio. "How me?"

I smiled with relief. "Loud and clear. Uh, how are you?"

"Feel like I got gobsmacked by a speeding truck. Otherwise, I'm great, boy."

"We're RTB. Olympus has you now. Good luck. We'll see you on the Boat."

We climbed into the dark, and Pop was on his own.

"He'll be okay," Kyra said.

"Yeah." I shrugged off my doubts to face my new fear of flying alone in the dark. "He'll be fine."

"It's us I'm worried about right now."

"What? Why?"

"We are seriously low on go juice. That was an expensive diversion, we have to give the rescue operations at the *Trenton* a wide berth, and our dinged-up wing is killing our fuel efficiency. I'm surprised the wing is still on the jet."

As I climbed onto the tanker's track at angels twenty, I decided to imitate Pop's cool. "Don't worry about a thing. Texaco, coming right up."

Only we couldn't find it. I checked my thigh boards and confirmed we were in the right place. But it wasn't here. It was gone.

This was not normal. This was very, very wrong.

I changed radio frequency and called Olympus.

"Wait, one," she said.

Medusa had other problems to deal with. While I wasn't happy being put on hold during a very important call to my life line, I was developing a fresh respect for the grump. She was handling an enormous task load that included a mounting list of crises, and if she had her own helmet fire, she wasn't showing it.

Finally, she came back on. "Go ahead."

"Tanker posit?"

"Wait, one ... No sweet tankers in your area." The tanker had run dry or been diverted in the chaos of the Chinese attack, which made me wonder who else the enemy might have struck and where. "Say state."

I checked the fuel indicator and gulped. "Two-point-eight." Twenty-eight hundred pounds in the tank. We had around thirty, forty minutes of flying time left before we dropped out of the air, less if Kyra was correct about the damaged wing.

Surprised silence on the radio. "Your signal is max conserve and RTB now. I will contact Mother and declare an emergency, so expect your signal Charlie or an alert tanker to meet you in the air."

"Roger." Save gas and expect to land as soon as I got home, got it.

It was going to be real close and promised a varsity end to a high-varsity day. Remember what I said earlier about sweating fuel? I was doing that now.

Making things worse was when we arrived, well…

Mother wasn't there either.

Groaning, I checked the carrier's course on my thigh boards against my HUD readout. Again, we were in the right place. The Boat wasn't.

This was not good.

In fact, it was a nightmare. We were screwed.

For all the good luck we'd had during the fight against the Chinese, karma now seemed to be righting the scales in spades.

"Start dumping whatever we don't need," Kyra advised. "Everything."

I'd already punched off our empty drop tanks during the battle. "*Every*thing?"

"Everything."

This next part was painful. With the punch of a few buttons, I dumped more than ten million dollars' worth of high-tech missiles into the drink.

The jet felt lighter and more responsive. Reducing our load helped, but it didn't solve our biggest problem, as we couldn't RTB if we couldn't find our B to RT.

"Look at our eleven o'clock," Kyra said.

Glowing like a green coal in my night vision glasses, a blob of light shined in the darkness. "What *is* that?"

"It's Mother."

"What—?"

"She's been hit. She went evasive."

At least part of the flight deck was on fire, the blaze steadily shrinking as emergency crews fought to control it.

How? When? I'd find out later. That is, if I survived this. Right now, I had a more immediate problem.

I couldn't land the plane on a foul deck, and I couldn't talk to Mother.

God, EMCON sucked.

"We could try to signal them," Kyra said. "Find out if we can land."

"How? With our lights? I don't know Morse code, do you?"

Olympus popped onto the radio. "Vampire hit at home plate. Mother is on a new course. Stand by for instructions on emergency frequency."

"Roger, Olympus," I said. "And thank you."

I glided toward a lower altitude as I approached the ship. The fire steadily shrank and winked out, one good sign.

Mother next called us on the emergency frequency. As the enemy had already located the ship, the Captain had decided to allow some exceptions to EMCON. I'd never been so happy to hear Mother's voice.

My report on my low fuel state was met with a moment of silence. I didn't have enough gas to make it to any other tankers that might be up. I barely had enough to make a pass at the flight deck.

"Your signal is max conserve," Departure radioed. "Stand by."

No kidding, I thought. *Consider me conserving to the max.*

"They're going to tell us to ditch alongside the Boat," I told Kyra.

A controlled ejection over the sea at night.

I did not want to do that.

Kyra said nothing. She didn't want to do it either.

While the big wheels talked about what to do with me, Departure came back on to vector me into a holding pattern behind the ship.

"Come *on*," I growled. I had less than twenty minutes of flying time left.

"Take angels one-point-two, fly heading zero-one-zero," Departure instructed. "We are rigging the barricade. Stand by for your rep."

I didn't answer. *Barricade?* Surely, I hadn't heard her right.

The XO appeared on the line. "Good to hear your voice, Beaver."

"You too."

"Let's run this down. You carrying any ordnance or tanks?"

"Negative. I'm clean."

I answered the rest of his questions in a dream. The cockpit filled with the aroma of my flop sweat.

"The net is going up," he said. "The landing area is clean. You got this. The LSO will hold your hand the whole way down. Any questions?"

"Negative."

"Attaboy. I'll see you both on the deck. Stand by."

"It can't be true," Kyra said once I signed off.

"There's no other way to do it," I said. "Unless we punch out."

We barely had enough gas in the tank for a wave-off. We'd have one go at this.

So yeah, it was true. We were doing the barricade. I just hadn't imagined I'd ever have to land in one. All the senior aviators talked about how scary it was, though none of them had ever done it themselves.

Twenty feet high and stretching across the flight

deck, the barricade consisted of a web of interlocked nylon straps, the kind of net you might use to catch Moby Dick. In principle, the aircraft travels into the webbing and transfers its energy across it until safely stopping.

In practice, it's like flying an aircraft jet at over a hundred miles an hour into a really strong volleyball net.

Of course, hitting it isn't easy, either, as nothing ever is. You have to land precisely to avoid crashing, rolling off the edge, or barreling into parked jets. Even if you're right on the money, you risk damage to the plane that can kill you.

And oh yeah, if you screw up, you can't bolter. You can't even eject.

In terms of pucker factor, it's off the charts. I'd rather ditch.

The master caution light came on, spraying more gasoline on my helmet fire.

"Fuel, low," Bitching Betty twanged. "Fuel, low."

"Okay, Mom!" I yelled back at my console. "Let's just do this, then."

"Jack," Kyra said. "Jack?"

"What?"

"You got this. You do."

"Sure thing," I whispered in terror. "Piece of cake."

"Hey… You listening to me?"

I said nothing, lost in premonitions of fireballing on the deck.

"HEY, NUGGET."

I snapped out of my fugue. "WHAT?"

"I said you got this. So do it or I'll punch you."

I took a deep breath, snapping out of it. "Aye, aye, ma'am."

"Three-One-Oh, Paddles," the LSO said on the radio. "Let's get you home."

He rattled off questions, which helped me focus. Approach speed, weight, fuel state. Then we covered the procedure. Land the plane, cut the engines, roll into the net. Imagine somebody talking you off the ledge, only he's advising you to jump.

My console whooped. "Bingo! Bingo!"

It was Mom, nagging me again. A warning my fuel was at a critical level. A thousand pounds left. Only miles from *Independence*, I set up a straight-in while Kyra reviewed the ejection procedures in case the engines rolled back on us.

The LSO returned to guide me in. On Mother's dark flattop, I knew, sailors had rigged one state-of-the-art barricade between two raised stanchions.

I'd ride the ball all the way into the net.

"Dirty up!" Kyra's voice cut through my helmet fire.

"Right, right," I lowered the gear handle and set the flap switch. My Rhino buoyed on a brief rush of lift.

The glide slope indicator appeared on the HUD.

"It's just a night landing," Kyra said in the back. "Just another landing."

Her advice would have been comforting if night landings weren't already terrifying and I didn't suck at them. *Just a night landing* was usually enough to freak me out. I can't speak to whether foxholes turn atheists into believers, but I am certain night landings and barricades do wonders for the faith.

I was in the groove now, eyes on the ball.

"Three-One-Zero, Rhino, ball, one-point-zero."

"Roger, ball, twenty-six knots," the LSO said, calm and confident as always, as if this were a normal landing on a typical night.

Another deep breath, easy on the throttle to stay on speed, nudging the stick to keep the ball zeroed. The carrier appeared as a grainy smudge in the gloom. The LSO gently chided me with corrections on attitude, power, and lineup, walking me every step of the way down the glideslope.

The deck appeared, expanding by the second.

Sucking oxygen, I wrenched my eyes from the ball to gape at the barricade, rigged between the third and fourth arresting wires.

If I landed normally, I'd hit the goddamn thing.

Eyes wide and watery with terror, I returned my attention to the golden ball like Icarus mesmerized by the sun.

"Easy, EASY," barked Paddles. "Okay, you're on, you're on—!"

Ball, ball, ball—

"You're on—NOW CUT! CUT!"

Cowabunga!

WHAM!

The tires punched the deck. The net rushed toward me as my Rhino rolled straight into the webbing. The impact was like running into a brick wall, and then the wall backed away with you still mashed against it, like some kind of brutal cartoon.

Otherwise, I didn't see much, as I had my eyes clenched shut.

When I opened them, I was on the deck. I was

alive.

"You okay back there?" I said.

"Jesus, God!" Kyra swore. "Thank you, Jesus."

This time, we laughed our asses off. Laughed with relief.

I wasn't just lucky. I was blessed by God.

THIRTEEN

War kicks your ass.

A voice yanked me from fitful dreams of being chased by a malevolent PL-12 that dogged me all night like some kind of missile Terminator.

"Reveille, hotshot," Duke said again.

I was back in my stateroom. The piping over my bunk gurgled. The catapult clacked in the carrier's guts as it prepared to slingshot a jet into space.

Every wretched muscle I owned ached and felt stiff. Otherwise, I was happy to find myself safe in my stateroom aboard *Independence*.

"Okay," I croaked, feeling like something broken that the cat dragged in.

Duke banged on the frame. "You too, sunshine!"

"I'm up, I'm up," Snoopy said in the rack below mine.

My mind flashed to stumbling away from my jet into a group of sailors, who hustled me across the deck. The Air Boss yelled something over the 5MC. A medic checked me out. Back in the ready room, our squadron mates wanted to talk to me and Kyra, and I wanted to find out what was happening on the Boat, but I was too drained to do more than nod at the jumble of words pouring over me. The XO kept our debrief mercifully short and sent us to our racks.

Which were still here, thankfully, inside our staterooms, despite the missile attack. What had happened last night while we were away was this. China fired a wave of DF-21 and Wrecker missiles at *Independence* from mainland rocket bases. An AWACS plane staging from Guam detected the attack and radioed the fleet. Most of the missiles splashed harmlessly into the Pacific, as information about the carrier's whereabouts moved too slowly through the kill chain for the People's rocket forces to gain an accurate fix. Several more were destroyed by the carrier screen and the Boat's antimissile defenses.

Then no more appeared on the radar. Across the Boat, relief.

The attack appeared to be over.

Two Chinese submarines raised to launch depth and lobbed a missile each from a distance of thirty miles. The missiles skimmed the water as they approached. The Phalanx guns activated, and Mother released a hail-Mary burst of Pandarra Fog, a cloud of carbon fibers designed to blind missiles, in a hard turn to starboard.

It worked, mostly. One missile went stupid and submerged. The other became confused, zoomed up, and exploded near the flight deck.

The resulting explosion killed or wounded twenty-nine crew, rattled aviators and gear off the bulkheads of staterooms and ready rooms, and damaged five Super Hornets in the VFA-109, four of which were now a total write-off.

"Glad you made it aboard," Duke said. "Heard you had an adventure."

"Yeah." I plopped down to the deck and rubbed at eye glue.

"Go Navy. So what was it like?"

"A real leap of faith." I shuddered.

"Knowing you, you probably asked for it," the

WSO deadpanned. "You begged them to string it up so you could try it out."

I burst out in a laugh. "Shut up, Duke."

He chuckled. "Thank you for your service."

My laughter trailed away as I gazed over at Track's empty bunk. Overhead, a jet took off with a loud muffled roar and a thud that shivered down the bulkheads.

I didn't want to think about where Track was now, still strapped in his jet on eternal patrol at the bottom of the Philippine Sea. We weren't bosom pals or anything, but he was so good-natured it was hard not to like him. He loved reading and could be a real nerd about military history. One of those guys you could rib without it turning into a blood feud. In fact, I'm sorry to say, the last thing I said to him was a "your mom" joke.

My stateroom, which once felt like a cage packed with rats, seemed empty today. "Any word on Nine Lives and Pop?"

His own smile faded. "They picked up Nine Lives. As for Pop, they're still looking."

I turned away with a wince. "Shit."

He patted my shoulder. "Not everything's on you. We'll find him. In the meantime, you have just enough time to clean up and grab chow before the brief."

Pepsi Man stirred in his rack. "I feel like I slept five goddamn lousy minutes."

Snoopy grumbled his way to the sink to shave. "Maybe I'll get to do something today. Stuck on freaking desk duty while you guys fight a battle."

Poor Snoopy never could catch a break. Most of the time it was his own doing; he was so terrified of failure he ended up sabotaging himself. This time, it was just dumb luck he'd missed the action.

Pepsi Man grunted. "Next time, I'll sleep while you dodge missiles. Deal?"

"I was up half the night doing paperwork."

"The nugget has identified a *severe breach* of Navy protocol," he said, now completely awake and in full Pepsi Man mode. "I shall cable Washington."

Duke, however, offered a sympathetic nod. "Bum luck, Snoop. You should complain to the skipper. Tell him you want more flying time."

"You think so?"

"Sure, man. Always tell him how you feel. He loves feedback."

Then he tossed me a wink, and I couldn't help but laugh again. The United States was now in a shooting war with China, but Duke was still Duke.

Which was fine, as I suspected it was the little things that got you through war, as so many of the big things had a way of hurting.

Minutes later, we went to the Dirty Shirt for breakfast. We met Kyra and the Valkyries coming the other way down the passage. My WSO and I exchanged a cocky smile, and I gave her a high-five on the way into the wardroom, which we entered with just a little bit of extra swagger.

Ravenous, I filled my tray with bacon and eggs and a mug of coffee. The Gargoyles weren't scheduled to fly this morning and the skipper had called a meeting, so everybody in the squadron was there. I sat where I usually did with the junior officers, buffered from the senior aviators by the Valkyries. The seniors acknowledged me with nods, a casual gesture that today was loaded with meaning.

While I'd performed a varsity landing, varsity deeds are part of the job when you fly alongside the best. Still, what I'd done was not bad for a nugget.

I was already a Gargoyle, but I'd suddenly gained acceptance by a far more restrictive club. With these simple nods thrown my way, the senior aviators recognized me as one of their own. It felt absolutely righteous.

At the same time, it didn't feel like anything. After what I'd survived, their acceptance wasn't as important as it was when I woke up yesterday. Sometimes, the best part of admittance into the club is relief from wishing you were in it.

Besides that, I'd already gained a moment's acceptance from the guy who mattered most, which is the screwup I saw in the mirror every day. I hadn't let down my squadron. I'd done my part. I liked myself so far this morning. Yesterday's events seemed like a strange dream now, but I'd revisit them by reviewing the tapes that had recorded my HUD and attack displays.

On this high note, I cast a moony-eyed glance at Kyra, who'd developed a sixth sense for my pining. She caught my eye and smiled. I expected Rowdy to burst out with some loud remark, but she wasn't there. As if to honor her ghost, her usual seat was empty. Kyra caught the shift in my gaze, and her smile drifted away.

That's war. *You're* awesome, but somebody else is dead and gone.

Feeling strangely guilty, I went all the way to ruin my good mood. Snoopy asked me, Duke, and Pepsi Man about the battle, and I found myself doing a play by play that frequently dived into outright bragging about downing two jets.

Not that there's anything wrong with bragging among aviators. You wanted to be the best, and it usually helped if somebody *noticed* you being the best, and if they didn't notice, it subsequently sometimes helped if you *reminded* them. Today, though, it only made me feel strangely overexposed and guilty. Like a fake.

Track's dead, I thought. *And you're bragging.*

Always my own worst critic.

Pepsi Man and Duke started to talk over me about their own heroic exploits, and I yielded the floor to these Hectors.

"Make a hole." Tiger nudged a space across the table and bored his eyes into mine. The XO squeezed into the seat next to me. All conversation stopped.

The XO tucked into his eggs. "How are you holding up, Beaver?"

"Hunky-dory, XO."

"Good to hear."

Tiger said, "We need to hear about Pop. Everything you remember."

I explained the damage from the heat seeker, the engine problems, his decision to punch out, how he wasn't wounded by the ejection.

"Very well," he said.

Their inquiry didn't give me positive feelings about the success of Pop's recovery. "Skipper…"

He fixed me with a penetrating stare. "Something on your mind, Beaver?"

I shook my head. Whatever I needed to know, the skipper would tell me, otherwise, I'd grown at least wise enough not to bug him with questions he either couldn't answer yet or didn't know the answer to. "No, sir. I'm good."

"Attaboy. Now eat your breakfast before it gets cold."

My first "attaboy" from the skipper, and it was for keeping my yap closed.

After chow, we trooped to the ready room for an all-officers' meeting, which gradually grew noisier by the moment as the squadron filled it out. I poured a fresh mug of coffee and settled into my chair between Snoopy and Frog.

"I think something really big is gonna happen," Snoopy said.

I raised my eyebrows. "China declaring war on us wasn't big enough?"

"I mean an op. We are going on the offensive today, mark my words."

"Or they might give us a rest and let somebody else pull their weight."

He grinned. "It's all hands on deck now, amigo. You'll see."

I'd find out momentarily. Everybody had coffees and seats, and the skipper wasted no time in addressing the squadron, which quieted faster than ever. Whatever he had to tell us, we wanted to hear it loud and clear.

"We're on the clock, Gargoyles, so I'll make this quick," he said. "In case you hadn't guessed, the United States is now in a state of war with the PRC. Yesterday, the enemy delivered a limited but effective sucker punch. We lost good people. We'll mourn them. Pop is still missing. We'll find him. We took our punch. Today, we're going to punch back."

"Told you," Snoopy hissed near my ear. I nodded.

"First, Lieutenant Danby is here to fill us in on the big picture. Lieutenant?"

The intelligence officer swept onto front stage. "Good morning, all y'all. Here's the word of the day."

Her usual bright smile was nowhere to be found, an unsettling sight and another sign that shit was real now. "Yesterday, the PLAN sent two waves of J-15 fighters to engage elements of our squadron near the red line. This provided cover for an assault by H-6 bombers, which fired a spread of YJ-83 antiship missiles. Three of these struck the *Trenton* and sank her at 1630 along with five officers and ninety-one enlisted. She was the first American warship sunk since 1945."

While we growled in our seats, Danby pressed on. "Meanwhile, PLA missiles cratered runways at Guam and Okinawa to hamper air operations. Of course, we also got hit, and between that and the air engagement, we lost some fine people."

"We're gonna kick their ass!" somebody yelled out from the back rows, and we all roared until Tiger took a step forward, shaking his head with lips pursed.

Once we settled down, he turned to Danby. "Let's hear it."

"Yes, there's more," she said. "Around the same hour, our nation's satellite network suffered a major missile and cyberattack. From here on out, we'll be talking to Pearl and Washington in relays, like one big game of telephone, and we're gonna have to work around navigation issues caused by GPS unreliability."

We all fell into a shocked silence. The Navy had evolved to become an electronic, networked fighting force, and the Chinese had hit us where it hurt. Without satellites, we couldn't detect missile launches.

Danby finally offered a tight smile, but it came out nasty. "Now let's hear the good news. The PRC had hoped to sink us yesterday and knock America out of the war in one punch, but they didn't even come close, and Mother is raring to go. Within two days, there will be not one but *three* carriers here in the Philippine Sea, with another coming out of the Indian Ocean able to strike at China's bases in the South China Sea. We sank one of the submarines that took a shot at us, and our own submarines are now wreaking havoc. With combined forces and hopefully Australia and Japan coming in to lend us a hand, we'll have the capability to put a whole lot of hurt on the PRC while most of their attention and assets are tied up in the fight with Taiwan. But we don't need their help right now. Because you know what?

"Get ready, cuz here comes the pearl in the oyster. We located *Hunan*. That's where all y'all come in." Her old chipper smile returned like a sunrise, making us sigh. "Y'all are gonna sink the fucker for me."

Mouth dropped open at the news we'd be assaulting a Chinese battle group but also her cuss word, as we'd never heard her say anything saucier than *sure as Shinola* and *H-E-double toothpicks*. Judging by her turning scarlet, she seemed as surprised as we were. After a moment of shocked silence, we broke into wild cheering, and this time, Tiger didn't break it up.

In fact, the skipper's leathery face stretched into a bulldog grin. "Roger that, Lieutenant. Thank you for the big picture." He then gave us all a martial glare. "Heads up. We're going to assault and sink an aircraft carrier. We're going to put down anything else the PLAN throws in our way. And we're going to do it today. In ninety minutes, in fact, while our intel is still fresh."

I won't bore you with every single thing that was said, but the basic plan was the bulk of the air wing was going to attack the *Hunan* battle group while the depleted VFA-109 guarded *Independence*. The assault element consisted of four waves of Super Hornets supported by Growlers and Hawkeyes. The first two waves would knock the enemy's planes out of the sky. The third would strike any warships between the last wave and *Hunan* itself. The last wave would release missiles at the PLAN carrier and sink it; in this strike package, six fighters would carry air-to-ground missiles while two served as a screening escort.

While we would have preferred to do this at night, when we'd have a stronger advantage over the PLAN, that option simply wasn't viable. We had a fix on *Hunan*, she was retreating, and we had to strike now before we either lost her or she slipped away to safety behind the mainland's fighter and missile shield.

You'd think that after I'd experienced the naked terror of combat and witnessed war's cost, I'd be unhappy to hear we were attacking, but I grinned like the proverbial kid in the candy store.

All I could think was, *This is gonna be insane!*

Yes, war is terrifying. Yes, comrades had died, and I wasn't exactly thrilled I'd taken the life of some dumb jock like me, and it was slowly dawning on me that I might die too. At the same time, combat had proved a rush unlike anything I'd ever experienced.

That one soaring moment where you get inside the enemy's turn circle and release weapons and swat him out of the sky in a flaming wreck, well, there's nothing like it in the world. Right or wrong, good or bad, whatever: Nothing compares to that single supreme moment of elation.

At this moment, all I could think about was getting back into the thick of it.

Ninety minutes. The skipper had warned us we were on the clock, and he wasn't kidding. Not a lot of time to prepare, as a big operation like this required understanding of its particular radio procedures, marshal and rally points, recovery, fueling track, and all the rest. But as I said, our situational awareness was diminished with the loss of key satellites, so we had to act fast if we wanted to bag the elephant.

A strident call from the back of the room: "ATTENTION ON DECK."

We leaped out of our chairs and stiffened to attention as Captain Vaughn stomped through the ready room to take the stage. No, he wasn't the Boat's captain. While the floating end was his domain, Vaughn's was the flying end. He was the *commander, air wing*, though the designation used to be *commander, air group*, and the Navy loves tradition, so that's what we called him, the CAG.

The CAG was one of those guys we junior officers all wanted to be, as he was the best. Vaughn didn't just graduate from TOPGUN, he once taught it. He was a walking resume of countless carrier landings, combat missions, deployments, and a lot of tough days in cockpits and carrier control rooms.

While he couldn't guarantee our individual safety, we knew we couldn't lose with him in command.

The CAG regarded all of us with that glinty stare a hotshot gives when he recognizes his own. He wore a flight suit, as he'd be flying into combat with the air wing today. "Asses in seats. I don't intend to take up much of your time."

We complied, though we sat more or less at attention, and even the skipper and XO standing behind him assumed a formal pose, barrel chests puffed out and hands clasped behind their backs. Lieutenant Danby gazed at the handsome and rugged CAG like she wanted to devour him from his salt-and-pepper crewcut to his brown aviator boots.

"Gargoyles, you are about to fight in a historic operation. You'll—" He glanced at Tiger. "Did you give them the news yet?"

"I was just about to, sir," the skipper said.

"If you're okay with it, I'll do the honor." When the skipper nodded, Vaughn turned back to us. "I'll be leading the first wave, but as for you boys and girls, you get the grand prize. You'll be the last to go in, and you'll sink *Hunan*."

We cracked our own bulldog grins. We'd been hoping to hear just that.

"Listen to your CO, remember your training, and don't miss." He offered us all a proud and paternal smile. "Good hunting."

With that, the CAG left the room to wild applause and cheering as if he'd delivered the world's most dramatic speech involving mom, apple pie, the Fourth of July, and our sweethearts counting on us back home. He could have composed and orated the next Gettysburg Address right then, and it wouldn't have been as inspiring as his simple parting words.

Good hunting, a remark used to send aviators into combat since World War Two.

It meant, *You're the best war fighters on the planet, and you can only win.*

After the briefing, we crowded into the paraloft to gear up for the mission. Helmeted with nav bags slung over our shoulders, we hustled onto the catwalk hungry for payback and adventure.

The first thing we checked was how the weather felt. The sun was shining in the blue sky between thick patches of white cumulous clouds. A good day for flying. A moderate breeze blew from the west at twenty knots.

On the way to our jets, Snoopy raised his fist for a bump. "See you on the other side, Beaver."

I bumped his fist with mine. "You ready for this?"

"Spring loaded, amigo."

Spanky hurried over to get in on the fist-bumping action. "We're finally getting in the game, Snoop!"

Snoopy grinned. He wasn't missing out on this party, his big chance to prove himself and fill his dad's big shoes.

"The cute little nuggets are displaying martial bravado," Pepsi Man said as he and Duke strutted past, "when they should be watching and learning."

We responded with raspberries.

Eye-rolling stuff, I know. I've spared you most of the endless bonding that went on aboard the Boat, from inside jokes to singing hip-hop together like a bad movie trope. This was a real moment for us nuggets, though, as the squadron had been blooded and emerged the victor, and we felt like an elite force swaggering to our waiting Rhinos.

We were about to go into combat, and this confidence would be an asset. It's why we said *good hunting* instead of *try not to get yourself killed out there today.*

We never think what we say to people will be the last thing said.

Still chuffed and macho from the banter, I caught up to Kyra. "We're gonna need our A game today, Guns. Show Pepsi Man and Duke how it's done."

"This isn't a video game, Jack," she snapped. "You only get one life."

Bewildered, I said nothing. When Kyra called me Jack instead of Beaver, she was being extra serious, like somebody calling timeout to stop the game.

Holly Young welcomed us to the jet, but this morning she didn't appear her usual chipper self. She updated me on the status of the aircraft we'd be flying.

"Outstanding," I said and turned to Kyra. "What's with you?"

"I need you to take this seriously."

"I do. I will, I promise. I know it's personal to you."

"I said I hated the PRC. I didn't say I wanted a war."

I couldn't reconcile this with the ice-cold killer she became in the cockpit. "Are you okay?" Tears streamed from under her aviator sunglasses. "You're not okay."

"Sam's dead." Sam Riggs, our plane captain, all of nineteen years old.

I stood helplessly. "How?"

"He disappeared in the explosion," she said. "They think he went overboard."

The missile's detonation had apparently flung Sam off the flight deck to plummet ten stories into the sea, where he was left in the carrier's wake.

"Oh." It explained why the brown shirt had been so glum. It was a horrible way to die. "I didn't know."

"I can't believe I'm almost out, and a major war starts," she growled. "I just wanted to pay for college and fly airplanes. This shit will follow me the rest of my life."

"We'll be okay, Guns," I said, and I believed it.

I was right. We would be. She was right too, as it would turn out. The horrible shit really does follow you after the shooting stops.

Feeling sour now, I put my head down to focus on our jet, giving this everyday inspection extra care to ensure not a single fastener was loose. All the while, I winced and tried to swallow the lump in my throat. After dealing with Track, Dangle, and Rowdy dying, I'm not sure why Sam's death hurt so much. Maybe it was seeing how it affected Kyra, but I believe it was because Sam wasn't really a combatant. He didn't have a weapon. He was just a kid who fixed planes.

Satisfied our faithful jet would hold together in the air, we climbed into our cockpits, plugged in, and checked systems.

Holly returned to make sure I was buckled up good and tight.

"Sorry about Sam," I said. "I just found out. He was a good guy."

I expected stirring words like *avenge him* or *pay 'em back for me*, but she only muttered, "Thanks," and returned down the ladder.

"We'll be okay," I said again once she'd gone.

Kyra didn't respond this time either. But we would be okay, and today, we'd pay them back.

Our Super Hornet had a different weapons loadout

for this op. In addition to Sidewinders on the wing-tips, we carried six AGM-65 Mavericks. The Weapons Department had assembled them in the magazine and transported them up a special elevator to load them like monstrous packages for special delivery.

Holly walked me through the startup sequence. I cranked the motors and fired up the engines. When it was our turn, we taxied to take tension at the catapult.

Then bang, we burst down the track, reality blurring around the deck's edge straight ahead. With a final thump, we were off the bow and back in the war.

I grabbed the control stick and cleared. The Super Hornet felt heavy with all the missiles under its wings. At ten miles, we climbed to rendezvous with the rest of the squadron at twenty thousand feet. Together, we proceeded out of EMCON range, where the skipper radioed us for a roll call.

We sounded off. From left to right: Athena, Snoopy and Spanky, Pepsi Man and Duke, Tiger, me and Kyra, Smoke, Frog and Hotdog, and Sparky and Pointer.

This done, Tiger said, "Nightwing, Texaco is at our twelve o'clock for thirty miles, angels twenty."

We'd left *Independence* with most of our maximum takeoff weight in weapons, so we had to top up our fuel in the air before proceeding on mission. I'd like to simply tell you that we "gassed up and kept going," but this routine procedure deserves mention as a whole other kind of scary, kind of like a big dragonfly and an even bigger dragonfly mating in midair.

We gained a visual on the tanker and lined up for refueling. A very long and flexible hose protruded from the rear of the aircraft, terminating in a padded basket. One by one, we yo-yoed to take our turn connecting our probe into the basket while everybody else flew formation off the tanker. The connection has to be done at just the right rate of closure. For nuggets like me, even routine operations can be varsity events, and refueling is no exception.

Practice makes perfect, however, and I'd done it enough times that I was able to secure and maintain stable contact without holding us up from our op.

After topping up our tanks, we zoomed after the squadrons constituting the first two attack waves. We'd arrive around five minutes after the second.

I prayed they'd succeed not only because they were on my side but also because my mission success and even survival depended on it. Fully loaded out with antiship missiles, our jets were cumbersome and less maneuverable, and we had fewer air-to-air missiles if interceptors challenged us.

Our screening element—Athena out front on the left and Sparky on the right—would act as guarding escorts, ready to engage any enemy fighters that got in our way. They were good, but even they wouldn't be enough if the first two waves failed.

We'd either abort or end up flaming into the Pacific.

Black smoke smudged the horizon. A bright flash burst like lightning. Like a coming storm, only it was no storm but instead a battlefield.

"Oh, God," Kyra said behind me.

I had to agree: *Oh, God*, indeed.

We flew on, straight toward hell.

Like a violent twister, fighter planes tangled in a massive furball that swirled from near sea level all the way up to forty thousand feet. Another flash; a Flying

Shark corkscrewed toward a watery grave, almost taking out a Super Hornet along the way. Holed by anti-ship missiles, a Chinese destroyer blazed on the sea, surrounded by a vast, burning oil slick.

"Nightwing, arm hot, roll tape," Tiger radioed. "Buster."

We throttled to full power and roared to bypass the maelstrom of shrieking planes and flying missiles.

"Watch everything, look at nothing," he added. In other words, keep your eyes peeled and don't get distracted.

I'd been doing both, gawking at the terrifying war movie unfolding before me. We seemed to be winning the contest for air supremacy. Smelling blood in the water, my instincts screamed at me to veer toward the bandit cloud and pick off somebody who looked vulnerable, but we had a different mission.

We zoomed past the burning destroyer, which slowly sank by the stern in a massive fountain of foaming water, and then we had nothing but bright, cloud-patched sky ahead of us.

"Nightwing, tactical formation, line," the skipper said. "Tag target."

The formation unfurled into a wall of fighter jets racing to the horizon. Kyra called out she'd acquired a big surface target ahead.

Hunan.

"Prosecuting," Tiger reported to Strike.

My console alarmed the thermal signature of missile launches.

"Tally launch," Kyra called out, "nine o'clock low!"

I jerked my head and spotted the missile frigate

approaching from the south.

"SAM in the air," Athena radioed. Surface-to-air missiles. "FFG-X on our nine!"

"Snoopy is defending!" he called on the squadron common, electrifying me.

Smoke had eyes on the missile and hung back a little to watch and radio helpful instructions. The rest of us plowed ahead as ordered.

"Two in the air!" Smoke warned. "That's two on you, Snoop!"

My radar contact began to blink.

"Faded," Kyra said.

We were being jammed again. We'd briefed for this. Between the jamming and the GPS system high over our heads winking in and out of action, we'd do this old school, with eyes on the target.

But I wasn't thinking about that, I was thinking about Snoopy fighting for his life. Smoke chanted, *Break left! Throttle, throttle, throttle—*

"That's one down," Snoopy yelled.

You got this, I thought.

"I don't have enough speed, I'm—"

The transmission cut off and left dead silence in its wake.

"Status, Snoopy," Tiger said.

"Mayday," Smoke called. "Snoopy is hit. I don't see a chute."

"Copy that," Tiger said, his voice strained. "Nightwing, gate."

I throttled past full power and grunted as the world outside distorted into a circle surrounded by a blur. Once we were past the immediate threat, Tiger ordered us to reduce speed and drop altitude.

The loss of acceleration turned the anxious butterflies in my stomach into swirling fighter planes. We now flew in unison with the sea surging beneath us, and all I could think about was how Snoopy never could catch a break, and now he no longer existed.

Whoosh, he'd had gone defensive.

Seconds later, *bang*, he was hit.

Crash, he and his WSO were dead.

"Stay on it, Jack," Kyra said. "We got this. Everything else can wait."

I grunted as I forced my feelings aside. "Yeah. Roger that."

Hunan appeared on the horizon, just a smudge at first.

"Tally one CV, three helos, twelve o'clock," the skipper said.

"Roger," Sparky acknowledged and flew to attack the helicopters, which weren't a threat but in our way.

Seconds later, a helicopter burst into flame and tumbled into the water. He was knocking them down as if swatting flies.

"Stand by to shoot primary target," Tiger said. "Weapons tight until the order."

Sweating under my oxygen mask, I selected Mavericks from the STORES page. Ahead, *Hunan* grew larger by the moment. *Kuznetsov* class, seventy thousand tons at full loading, a thousand feet long.

The carrier showed us her stern as she tried to escape at thirty knots, leaving a long foaming track. A J-15 shot off her pronounced ski jump bow.

"Engaging," Athena called out as she veered to intercept.

In my head, I kept hearing the voice of one of the

fighters assaulting the Death Star in *Star Wars* chanting, *Stay on target!*

I chuckled into my mask, expelling the horror and stress I felt.

"Focus, Jack!" Kyra yelled from the backseat.

"I *am*, Kyra!" I yelled back.

Then I heard her muttering, "*Kill it, kill it, kill it—*"

"Pepsi Man, weapons free," Tiger said. "Target is the stern. Nightwing, stand by to turn to two o'clock for a broadside."

"Bulldog!" Pepsi Man whooped over the comms.

His six Mavericks streaked out on dramatic smoke trails toward the fleeing carrier. Eight feet long and weighing seven hundred pounds, the missiles rocketed ahead while we veered off for our broadside strike.

Focused on my maneuver, I craned my neck to quickly inspect the result. *Hunan*'s defensive systems had swung into action. Gatling guns rattled and air-to-air missiles spewed from their battery toward the incoming Mavericks.

Two exploded in the air. Then another.

The last three got through.

The Mavericks struck the carrier's giant propellers whipping the sea into rapids and produced a beautiful mushrooming fireball.

Pepsi Man whooped, and we all joined him. "Target hit!"

The carrier slowed to a crawl. J-15s sat on the deck, unable to launch.

"Splash one," Athena said with audible relief. She'd knocked down her bandit.

Moving as a single predatory organism, our formation pulled noses toward the carrier's starboard side and prepared for the main strike.

Fangs out, our Super Hornets screamed toward the target.

Hunan a big, fat, helpless target for our Maverick attack.

Tiger returned to the radio. "Nightwing, weapons free! Bulldog!"

I mashed the pickle switch on my control stick. "Bulldog!"

My airframe bucked as all six of my Mavericks detached from their mountings, rocket motors igniting. They joined eighteen others that streamed ahead of the formation toward the target.

"Olympus, Nightwing, bruiser," Tiger reported, letting the Hawkeye and battle watch captain know we'd shot our wad at the carrier.

Hunan's defensive systems reacted but were quickly overwhelmed by the strong assault. Thunder rent the air as the missiles struck the hull near the waterline, hurling debris and vast arcs of spray into the air.

"Goddamn," Kyra breathed at the flashes.

Goddamn was right. It was an incredible sight.

Massive black clouds mushroomed over the flaring hits, leaving the ship veiled in a wall of dust and smoke. The sea rushed into the gaping holes to flood compartments all along the starboard side, dragging the great warship into a groaning list. J-15s slowly skidded toward the edge as gravity fought their restraints.

"That's what you get!" Frog exalted.

After a roll call, Tiger radioed Strike. "Mission success. Target has a growing list and appears to be sinking. One plane is down, believed KIA but will mark posit and attempt to confirm. Winchester, RTB." Out of ammo and going home.

"Bravo Zulu, Nightwing," the battle watch captain congratulated us. "RTB."

Hunan was dying.

The carrier continued to list in a spreading circle of churning foam. Sailors floundered in the water. A Flying Shark slid down the deck to splash and disappear in the undulating sea. An avalanche of tumbling aircraft and gear followed.

Continuing our wide arc around the sinking ship, we headed for home.

The massive aerial confrontation was over by the time we returned. The Flying Sharks *Hunan* had been able to get in the air were either on the bottom of the Philippine Sea or had fled the fight. Several American fighters buzzed like angry hornets around the Chinese missile frigate, which died in a series of explosions that lifted the warship out of the water before tossing it aside in burning pieces.

The Chinese were tough, but the full power of American military might was on display today in a devastating blow.

War kicks your ass. This time, it kicked the PLAN's ass. The PRC had sowed a whole lot of whoopass, and they'd just reaped it.

Though not without cost to our side. Smoke circled the site of where Snoopy and Spanky went down but found no signs of survival. The XO confirmed them as KIA, a sobering finish to a climactic, triumphant victory.

Then we flew home and landed, as if this were all just another day's work. There, we were greeted with another big victory: Pop had been found, proof that while war is the worst of times, some of its moments can be the best of times.

FOURTEEN

"Why did you fight us, Prisoner 2299?"

You may recall asking me this, Deputy Bureau Chief Zhang Fang. This was before the trial started. We were in the interrogation room decorated with old Maoist quotes painted yellow against lurid red walls. You sat behind a table on the raised platform. The table was covered in white table cloth. Perched next to you, a minion wearing big glasses recorded our session.

I sat on a chair in the middle of the carpeted floor. Flanking the door behind me, two toughs in blue uniforms and peaked caps stood guard.

I was hesitant to repeat my name, rank, and serial number yet again. By this point, I'd been clubbed, kicked, electroshocked, waterboarded, sleep-deprived, dosed with red pepper in the eyes, and forced to run in chains and endure painful positions such as military crouches for hours.

I could barely sit in the chair. Even breathing hurt. There's a saying in the military, *make pain your friend.* Screw that. I wanted to take my pain and kill it with fire.

"You go first," I said.

You threw me *the look*, the one that said, *I could just order the guards to shove bamboo up your ass instead.*

"I'm not messing with you," I pointed out. "It's an honest question."

Your country sacrificed so much to first attack Taiwan and then throw your best sucker punch at America to keep us out of your war. You now suffer crippling sanctions, a crashed currency, angry neighbors, civil unrest, foreign investment drying up, hyperinflation, hunger.

Decades of progress, undone in just a few months. All that diplomacy to build good will since the 1970s, only to become an international pariah.

I really wanted to know why. I might be the only American to learn the truth.

"All Chinese people long for the Great Reunification," you told me. "It is our highest and purest national interest and the irresistible trend of the age."

"No, seriously. Why?" What you'd told me was just propaganda.

"It is the national dream. China dream. One China."

I glanced at the dweeby dude recording our session and understood that you couldn't speak freely. Everything you said went into the permanent record.

You couldn't say Taiwan—the Republic of China (ROC), what you call Chinese Tapei—challenged your Party's legitimacy. You couldn't say you wanted to break the reverse Great Wall of islands holding back your country's ambitions as a Pacific superpower, control all the bordering seas, dominate Asia, and always get your way and never be called out for it, like some kind of colossal man-baby.

Maybe it was one of these things, maybe it was all of them. I'd never know the truth. No American would ever know the truth—nor even the vast majority of your own people—because, no offense to Mao or anything, but your Party is full of shit, and its bullshit is the only truth that is allowed to be spoken or even thought. You couch it all in flowery language and philosophical framing like *cardinal virtues*, but however you put it, it's still a Great Wall of bullshit.

"You do not understand," you said, as if reading my thoughts. "This is a national yearning, a singular longing. Our untiring struggle to return Chinese Tapei to the People will go on until accomplished, even if it takes a century."

That's when I realized you weren't being politically correct. You actually believe it. You all do. You'll lick your wounds, make nice when it becomes convenient to do so, bide your time, and then try again. To you, America and the Taiwan Strait are your Berlin Wall, the only things holding China back from reunification.

"Your turn," you said.

"Why did I fight? You do know you attacked us, right?"

"You shot down our planes first."

"Suicide by American. Your aviators were hotdogging."

You shook your head. "It does not matter. Your presence in our territorial waters made war regrettably inevitable. What were *you* fighting *for*?"

I thought about it. I didn't fight for Taiwan. I mean, I like Taiwan and all that, I guess, but deep down I don't care about it and any promises we'd made, vague or otherwise. If it were up to me, they'd take care of their own problems. And it's hard for many Americans to say they cared about the poor people of Taiwan either when a wave of violence against Asian-Americans happened back home during the fighting, including firebombing of Chinese restaurants and vandalism in urban Chinatowns, and with many of the victims being of Taiwanese descent.

The US government certainly cared enough to fight a war, using a far more arcane, amoral, and realpolitik calculus involving geopolitics, historic alliances, resources, shipping lanes, the grand chess game, and the clash of twilight and emerging superpowers. The simple version appeared to be the competition of nations over resources disrupted business, and business produced jobs and prosperity, so wars have to be fought to maintain markets. One of the first things I'd learned about Taiwan was around ninety percent of the world's most advanced computer chips and about a third of its semiconductors are made there.

Beyond a *my team is the best team* kind of pride, though, I really didn't care about the United States being the world's bully cop or computer chips or guaranteeing the security of the seven seas to make the world safe for capitalism, not enough to fight and die for it, anyway. It wasn't like all that gushing prosperity was reaching me or anybody else I knew.

Then I had it. I fought for human liberty. Nobody deserves to suffer under a dystopian dictatorship lacking in even basic freedoms, including you, comrade. Well, it's true the Navy functions as an authoritarian dictatorship, but I volunteered for it, and I did it so my countrymen could have real freedoms. Every human being has rights, and your government stomps on most of them. Crushing Tibet, controlling speech and religion, rounding up Muslims in camps, scrubbing the internet of every view contrary to the Party line, organ harvesting from political prisoners, the *Black Mirror*-style Social Credit System—to a Westerner, it's the stuff of George Orwell and nightmares.

But did I really fight for that? In an abstract sense, sure, but if China is suddenly Nazi Germany, then why did our corporations ship our jobs to your country for decades with the government's blessing, offering our workers cheap foreign junk as consolation for low wages? Low wages that devastated small towns and forced guys like me to join the military because I had no other prospects for the future? Why did we send all that wealth to China, which your government used to finance one of the world's most powerful militaries I later had to fight?

Maybe I'd fought for far more personal reasons, then. A small part of me had spoiled for a scrap. I was a hammer, see. A finely crafted, very expensive, precision hammer, and hammers pray for nails because that's what hammers do. I wanted to face death and walk away. I wanted to be tested and see what I was really made of as a fighter pilot and a man. Lying in my rack at night, I fantasized about dogfights as much as I fretted about dying. I thought I'd become a hero and prove to myself once and for all that I wasn't a screwup.

But that's not what I fought for. While it had made me willing to fight, it wasn't the cause for which I'd fought.

You stared at me with endless patience, awaiting my answer.

"Survival," I said, though in an instant I knew this was a lie. "No. Yes."

"Explain."

"I fought for the people next to me. I fought for my tribe. I fought for their survival as if it were my own, just as they fought for me."

This brotherhood was the beauty of the shared experience of combat in war. I didn't add I'd also fought to avenge them when they died. That I'd fought for payback in a cycle of violence. Part of the ugliness of war.

Both are a duty that never really leaves you, even when you're a prisoner and your war is all but over.

FIFTEEN

So back to the war—wait up, you say, there's more to it? The story should be over! I'd arrived a dumb nugget, proven myself a capable fighter, won the acceptance of my tribe, and earned the affection of a tough and beautiful woman, right out of an '80s action movie. If it all ended there, this would be a happy and satisfying tale, the kind of story you catch on Netflix to unwind and enjoy some wish fulfillment.

But that's not how it went down. What happened for me right after the sinking of *Hunan* was… honestly, not a hell of a lot at first. As a rule, life in the Navy is generally hurry up and wait with endless busywork to fill up the waiting part and keep you primed to do some hurrying. We were at war, true, but war can be pretty boring most of the time, long stretches of tedium punctuated by minutes of terror.

We sank *Hunan*, and *Theodore Roosevelt* and *Ronald Reagan* finally showed up. In response, the PLAN pulled in its horns and retreated to the East China Sea, which the PRC had declared off limits to American, Australian, Japanese, and British warships. Taiwan's eastern coast now being relatively safe, previously idle cargo ships sailed into Suao Harbour to deliver military and humanitarian aid and haul away refugees and computer chips.

Meanwhile, China continued air and missile strikes across the island and lobbed a few bombs every day at Okinawa and Guam. Steaming out of the Indian Ocean, *Abraham Lincoln* suffered hits in a submarine ambush and withdrew, but not before its air wing blasted China's artificial islands into glowing cinders. Australia was in the game and providing support, and Japan edged closer to committing to the fight and teaching its bully neighbor a sharp lesson about respecting borders and international laws.

That's all I knew at the time, most of it courtesy of Lieutenant Danby's chipper intelligence briefs. For a guy living on a platform that projected power across the global stage, my world was pretty small, largely consisting of the cockpit, ready room, Dirty Shirt, Nest, infrequently visited laundry, and my own depressing stateroom with its three empty racks. While all this was going on, I sortied, flew the CAP, worked the duty desk, and took my turn as tower flower under Air Boss Donato's hammer gaze, but aside from chasing radar contacts that fled like phantoms, I wasn't doing much in the hurrying department.

Which was not enough for us hothead jocks of the Gargoyles, who'd bagged an elephant and wanted more. Victory is like downing eight cups of coffee, leaving you buzzing and wired and a little strung out. Of course, I had no idea the final showdown rapidly approached my face like a bucket of water followed by a brick.

The big battle started as it always did with something mundane, though in this case thankfully not embarrassing for me. This time, it was breakfast in the Dirty Shirt, where we armchair admirals shared our theories searching for the holy grail of knowledge—what would happen next? What did it mean for us?

Over bacon, flapjacks, and coffee, we talked about the ship's plan of the day, which promised the same boring routines, and wondered if there was still a war on.

"Maybe it's over, and we just don't know it yet," Duke said to rile up the rest of us JOs. He smiled as everybody started shouting, mission accomplished.

"Typical view from the backseat," Frog chortled as he slurped his coffee.

"Hey, watch it!" yelled Hotdog, his WSO.

"Now, now," Pepsi Man interjected, giving his fork a professorial wave. "Duke's sorry lack of martial acumen *aside*, he may be correct about the combat operational picture in that the present force allocation has achieved its primary mission objective."

"Which means what?" I said, egging him on.

"Which means the politicians are in the game and *we* are on the bench."

Frog almost sprayed his coffee. "Wang is still dropping bombs on Taiwan! We're still being hit at Guam and Okinawa—"

"Bargaining chips, my good man. You have my assessment."

I soured, as Pepsi Man's reasoning made sense to me. Our current posture was defensive, and we'd been told we'd only act if attacked again. We grew quiet as we pondered a war that was fizzling out almost as soon as it had ignited.

"Let's hear the gung-ho view," Duke said. "What do you think, Beaver? Any theories?"

I'd taken to agreeing with him and Pepsi Man on reflex. While we hadn't exactly become friends, the loss of three of our roommates had fused us into an even tighter-knit tribe that guarded each other's six at all times.

I was feeling aggressive this morning, though, and wanted to stir up my own ruckus. I was living in the shadow of a vast number of rockets itching to blow me into my constituent atoms if only they could get a fix on me.

"I think we're going to take it to the next level," I answered Duke with a carnivorous grin. "Knock them down so hard their people overthrow the CCP."

"Jesus, what do you mean?" Frog said. "We're gonna use nukes?"

"Who needs nukes?" I answered. "We have four carriers. We sank one of theirs. We wiped out their South China Sea islands. Now we're gonna hit them on the mainland."

"Wow. Jeez." He blinked. "You really think so?"

Pepsi Man nodded sagely. "The noble nugget has made a very *able* assessment built on the *finest* tradition of wishful nugget thinking."

"We sank *Hunan* and three other warships in a single afternoon, not to mention all the aircraft we shot down or destroyed on deck," I said. "You said it yourself a while back. The PLA is a paper tiger."

He didn't answer, for once at a loss, which I took as a victory. I'd learned the best way to shut him up was to quote him back to himself.

In the ensuing vacuum, every JO now offered opinions. Grinning at the shit storm I'd whipped up, I shot a look at Kyra. She was already gazing my way radiating the ol' stink-eye, which she did when I tried too hard to impress my squadron mates.

Pop walked past to police his tray, and I called out to him. "Hey, Pop! Settle an argument."

He paused to give me the half-annoyed, half-amused stare that senior aviators give nuggets who are feeling their oats. "What are you boys arguing about?"

"What do you think we'll do next? Are we going to hit the mainland, or do you think the PRC will call it quits?"

Pop turned thoughtful. "I know exactly what's gonna happen." He walked over to clap his hand against my shoulder. "You ready for this?"

Eyes boring into mine, he waited for a dramatic pause and added, "We're gonna go where they send us, when they send us."

Everybody laughed, thankfully drowning out my blustering and failing attempt at a witty retort. That's when the 1MC sounded overhead.

"FLIGHT QUARTERS, FLIGHT QUARTERS. MAN ALL FLIGHT QUARTERS STATIONS. SET CONDITION ONE-ALPHA FOR FLIGHT OPERATIONS."

Our eyes went wide as we regarded each other.

Pop looked up at the overhead and sighed. "When they send us."

Completely spring loaded, I'd been about to whoop at the sudden excitement, but seeing the senior aviator react with such a high level of chill gave me just enough pause to put a cork in it.

Yeah, maybe we were about to sink another carrier, no big deal. We were the varsity squad, after all. Just another day's work. I let my body language do the talking, adding some extra swagger as I tramped out into the passageway with all the other aviators to report to our ready rooms.

Another strike was in the works, the biggest one yet.

By now, you know the routine. Intelligence update. Short window of opportunity. New mission. Detailed breakdown. Suit up and go fast, with little time to learn the plan designed for the scenario now developing. A few inspiring words.

Only this time, the mission was to sink not a major warship but an armada. A massive fleet of seventy landing ships and helicopter- and hovercraft-bearing platform docks, scores of military support vessels, and hundreds of civilian boats converted to military use. All on their way to land hundreds of thousands of PLA troops on Taiwan's west coast, while airborne troops dropped around Tapei and other troops assaulted the heavily fortified Kinmen, Matsu, and Penghu islands.

This time, the mission involved a joint strike by not one but three American carrier air wings, supported by elements of the US, Japanese, Australian, and what was left of the Taiwanese Air Force. An assault with multiple waves involving hundreds of fighters and support aircraft, all tasked with a single mission—destroy as many transports and planes as possible. My air wing was at the center of the vast attack, flying feet dry over Taiwan to engage the enemy.

This time, we wouldn't be facing the limited power of an outclassed Chinese carrier group but instead the full wrath of the PLAAF. At full strength, some fifteen hundred fighters, from J-10 Firebirds to Su-27 Flankers to small numbers of the vaunted J-20 Mighty Dragons, none an easy pushover for our Rhinos, as I actually didn't believe the PLA was a paper tiger. A whole hornet's nest of them swarming across the strait to support the invasion.

This time, America was in it all the way without

any hemming or hawing.

And the battle we'd fight would likely decide the war.

As we crowded toward the paraloft, Lieutenant Danby flashed her pearly whites at each of us as we went in.

"You got this, Smoke... Go get 'em, Athena... Good hunting, XO... You come back to me safe, Beaver, y'hear?"

I smiled back. "Yes, ma'am."

The paraloft filled with aviators chattering about the mission and jostling each other as they pulled on gear. Helmeted and harnessed, I headed up to the flight deck behind Pepsi Man and Duke. No fist bumping this time, as we didn't need it. We'd all met the elephant, and we'd smacked the bastard. Nonetheless, a pit in my stomach started to yawn, and my legs trembled a little with pre-show jitters.

"Hey, guys," I said.

Duke cocked an eyebrow. "Yeah?"

I started to tell them to stay safe but stopped in time. "Good hunting."

Then Pepsi Man surprised me. "The nugget *will* be careful out there, or he'll answer to his betters. Copy?"

Duke nodded. "Foreal, Beaver. Come back in one piece."

"I will," I said, flustered and unsure what the right response was to this display of genuine feeling. "You too, guys. I mean it."

Then I jumped in surprise as somebody swatted my ass.

"Let's go, flyboy," Kyra said as she walked past.

I grinned and gave chase. "Aye, aye!"

We reached our trusty jet and started the preflight inspection.

I said, "You seem raring to go this time."

"Resigned, not raring," she replied. "This is happening whether I like it or not, so I want it over with. But yeah. Anybody who wants to get in the way of me making it home is gonna get murdered today."

My warrior queen.

We settled into our cockpits, from which I surveyed the seemingly chaotic flight deck toil under the misting gray sky.

The atmosphere could only be described as electric. This was it, the big showdown between the eagle and the dragon.

For this op, again everybody was flying, requiring all hands on deck. Air crews swarmed among grease-splattered aircraft, preparing them for launch with determined precision.

The first jets roared down the track. Then it was our turn to slingshot off the deck, and I punched the burners until *Independence* disappeared in our rear-view.

We lofted into the soup. The Super Hornet trembled on air pockets. Moisture beaded across the canopy and sprayed from the wings, blasted by the wind of speed. On the Strike frequency, Medusa fed us a steady stream of information about our bomber wave approaching from Guam, which we'd screen.

Then we broke the tops and found ourselves in brighter sky threaded by patches of gray murk, where we gassed up at a tanker. At the assembly point, the squadron established radio contact with each other and Strike, and we formed up in echelon as Tiger ordered.

The Japanese and the US Air Force assets at Okinawa would feint toward the Chinese fleet straddling the East China Sea, sucking at the PLA's air reserves, and then bombers would smash it with the goal of sinking as many ships as possible.

While this occurred, *Ronald Reagan*'s squadrons would sweep over the northern part of the island to strike the invasion fleet landing troops at the beaches around Taoyuan and Tapei. *Independence*'s squadrons would fly over the southern part to rip into the transports approaching Tainan. Then *Theodore Roosevelt*'s fighters would come up the strait for a southerly *coup de gras*.

We were producing contrails that marked our position, so we adjusted altitude. I was still trembling in my seat, only this time it wasn't air pockets, it was me. My bowels clenched, and my eyes started to boresight with tunnel vision. I took yoga breaths to try to calm down.

In war, both hurry up and wait are fertile ground for pants-shitting, but in aerial combat, you're so busy staying alive in your live videogame you actually forget how terrified you are, and it arrives later like a sucker punch. When it came to fear, I found the wait to be worse than combat.

I leaned into it hard. I didn't wonder what the Chinese aviators were thinking in their cockpits as they raced to our meeting on a battlefield of air. I didn't picture them as dumb twentysomethings like me, hoping to rewrite their stories to become heroes. They weren't even obstacles in the way of me making it back safe. They were outright evil for what they'd done to Snoopy and my other comrades, and I was going to kill them all.

I wasn't here merely to survive. I was hunting.

The dark, gauzy veil began to thin like waking from a dream. As we zoomed farther west, the skies cleared into patches of fast-moving gray-white clouds rolling across a sky the color of a bruise. A gray smudge appeared and spread across the horizon. We'd reached Taiwan, which grew larger by the moment.

Minutes later, we went over the beach, fangs out and cleared to kill.

After cresting the lush green Central Mountain Range dominating the eastern half of the island, Taiwan's great coastal cities spilled before us, bleeding dozens of smoke plumes from missile strikes. Desperate Republic of China F-16s and PLAAF fighters swirled and jockeyed over this nightmare.

Visible through a dissipating veil of morning fog, transports covered the strait arriving with troops or leaving to get more, some of them smoking as they sank from mines the sweepers had missed, missile strikes, or submarine torpedoes.

A thick black haze covered the shoreline. As we grew closer, sparks burst along the beaches as PLA troops charged valiantly to their deaths against what we'd been told was a brutal wall of mines, traps, spiked pits, barbed wire, and pre-sighted machineguns and artillery. The Taiwanese had prepared for this for seventy years, and they massacred the PLA by the hundred even as the beachhead steadily gained ground due to the assault's sheer weight.

I thanked Hermes I was up here instead of in that hell, though I was about to have my own problems.

One of our sister squadrons peeled away into a

dive through a knot of clouds to smash the beachhead while we pressed on toward the transports in combat spread formation, challenging the PLAAF to fight. My displays lit up with contacts before they started to blink and skip.

The battle had already started on the electromagnetic spectrum. Soon, I'd be it in all the way as the world's two greatest superpowers kicked the crap out of each other along a three-hundred-mile front.

Gargoyles started to call out tallies on approaching bandits, a whole lot of Chengdu J-10 Firebirds and J-6 drones and Su-27 Flankers and other aircraft. A pucker factor that was off the charts, though my blood was up and I was more eager than scared.

They're coming, I thought. *Let's do this.*

With a standoff advantage denied both sides, we were about to clash in an old-school, close-quarters air battle. As the first PLAAF fighters crossed the beach, Taiwanese SAMs rose from the countryside on smoke trails and claimed the first kills. A few planes broke off to attack the batteries. The rest came right at us as if enraged.

We raced to a head-on merge, my training overriding my growing helmet fire as I took in a vast amount of information all at once and converted it into geometry. One of the J-10s roared up to meet me. I grabbed an AIM-120 just as my radar changed frequency to counter the jamming and showed a target lock.

"Fox Three!"

The missile unlimbered with a *whump* and ignited, a blinding fireball that sped off with crackling thunder in its wake. The Firebird dumped its nose to dive, but the missile pivoted and looped down toward its prey.

I snap rolled to watch it chase the PLAAF jet and explode above the cockpit, sending it into a fiery corkscrew descent.

I didn't see a chute. A clean kill, an example of what happens when design, reflex, and luck come together just right.

Slightly dazed by this quick victory, I called it in on the radio. The squadron's first kill was mine.

Then I rolled the other way to try to find Pop, but it was impossible to discern his aircraft among the dozens now murdering each other in a massive furball. The battle's nucleus appeared to suck every fighter toward it like a tornado building in fury until it stretched from the ground almost to the stratosphere, occasionally spitting out a flaming wreck.

The bigger the air battle, the smaller the action, and this one had very quickly devolved into every pilot for him or herself.

The radio streamed observations, status, warnings, and kill claims. My immediate goal was to stay out of the bandit cloud, as my objective here wasn't to engage but attack. I scanned for an opportunity and zeroed on a juicy target when Kyra started chanting over and over that an Su-27 Flanker was plunging onto our six and overtaking us fast.

I wanted to see for myself, as the reaction I wanted to try might turn the tables or cook our goose depending on what the Flanker was doing, but I trusted Kyra as if her eyes were mine. I jerked the control stick to break into a high-G barrel roll that bled off knots and positioned the bandit in a high crossing-angle situation.

If he was coming at us too fast and close, the Flanker would overshoot. If not, I'd just handed him a golden opportunity to turn a capitalist into swiss cheese on burnt toast.

The Flanker zoomed past, and now it was my turn to be the bastard, but he peeled off in the opposite direction, and I sensed where this was now headed, which was a scissors fight, two planes weaving intersecting sine waves.

By the time our noses turned hot, we'd be too close for missiles, and that meant only one solution, which was to go to guns, usually the aviator's last weapon of choice but in cases like this the first.

Hicking my way through the turn, I selected my Vulcan cannon, read the geometry, and willed the tiny pipper on my HUD to line up with the target, which was a small but steadily expanding black dot.

"If you see a chance to bug out, take it," Kyra advised. "This is bullshit."

"I got this." Just one pass, and then I'd try to exit the fight.

The Flanker screamed toward my jet in a high-speed merge. We fired our guns at the same time. I'd read the geometry a little better than him—another case where superior training makes all the difference in real combat—and he was on my plane of attack while I was above his. His tracers strobed beneath my right wing, and he struggled to correct as I squeezed my trigger to lead my fire in bursts toward his cockpit. Then both Kyra and my threat alarm system yelled in my ear.

"Break left! Missile in the air!"

I yanked us into an organ-crushing ninety-degree turn and throttled up to rush roaring into the sun's heat and light, which I prayed would flood the heat-seeker's detector with background infrared. My G suit inflated with compressed air and pressed against my thighs and lower torso. Then I banked again and throttled down while Kyra dropped flares in our wake.

The heat-seeker went for it and exploded behind us with no damage.

"J-10 on our six!" she howled now. "And the Flanker's coming back at nine o'clock high! Jack, Jack, *Jack, Jack—*"

That was the problem with surviving a missile attack; while you jockeyed and twisted and ultimately triumphed, the enemy enjoyed plenty of time to climb onto your back. By now, it felt like everybody was gunning for my ass, making me wonder for the first time if we were winning this thing, though I didn't have the luxury of being able to ponder it because I'd opened the throttles again and dumped my nose into a shrieking dive.

The Firebird howled after me in hot pursuit, its pilot trying to get me back in his envelope for a second missile launch.

My jet didn't have the energy for another fancy turnabout play, especially with the Flanker still above us somewhere, so I had only one choice at the moment, which was to turn so as to mess with the J-10's crossing angle, aspect, and range.

I tipped my wing in a hard bank with my cockpit facing the enemy, though my enemy right now wasn't this Chinese hotdog but his missiles and gun.

The J-10 turned with me in a lag pursuit, letting me know he wasn't going to do me any favors and I'd have to get out of this myself, so I kept at the turn. I was in serious trouble now, stuck in a descending defensive spiral where I tried to weasel onto his six and he worked to stay on mine, a knife fight in a phone booth. Kicking myself the whole way down because I should have listened to Kyra.

We passed fifteen thousand feet and then ten. Below us, a bank of puffy stratocumulus clouds offered brief sanctuary and maybe an opportunity. My turn ate up my energy as fast as my descent could produce it. In the battle for aspect, my underpowered Super Hornet was slowly losing.

Trusting Kyra to keep an eye peeled for the Flanker, I pushed our jet to squeeze a tighter turn radius until the airframe began to buffet and my world started to tunnel to a grainy circle. Kyra yelled something, probably that I was an asshole and to stop fooling around with the seventeen-ton jet before I broke it and killed us both. I was taking us right to the edge over which I might lose control or gray out, which would be game over either way, but I needed this pilot to work as hard as possible for aspect and to boresight on this task.

Down and down we went all the way to seven thousand feet, and then we were in the cloud, which offered me a slim chance to turn the tables on him.

I jerked the stick in the opposite direction to exit the spiral. As we emerged gasping from the cloud, the Su-27 I'd lost earlier appeared overhead, about to overshoot and offer me position for a quick missile shot.

Before I could react to this bonus stroke of fortune, the pilot incredibly hotdogged into a falling leaf maneuver to try to brake and drop altitude right onto my six. My mouth dropped open at the sight of it.

Only he flubbed it.

During the controlled stall, the Flanker started to spin on its yaw axis, nearly out of control. If its pilot recovered from his mistake, I'd worry about him later, but he wasn't in my weapons parameters and now that he'd done my job for me, I had a bigger fish to fry.

Maintaining my heading, I looped back toward my J-10 pursuer and steeled myself for a head-on, guns-blazing merge.

The Firebird came out of the cloud still thinking he was on my tail. Instead, he found me charging him nose hot and already shooting. My rotary cannon rattled like a deafening martial drumroll.

My first burst of twenty-millimeter rounds shot past him. Then the pipper lined up center mass, and the second burst smashed his nose and wing. Pieces broke off and tumbled away in meteoric spray under the blistering gatling fire, as beautiful as it was horrible.

Breathing hard, I wrenched the stick to steer clear and zoomed past.

"He punched out," Kyra said. The pilot would land somewhere among the horrific fighting below. "The Flanker's still going down. Not bad, not bad." She blew out a massive sigh. "So what do we do now?"

Trembling from excess adrenaline and drenched in sweat, I checked my fuel indicator, which informed me we still had a little playtime if we wanted it, and besides, we still had some missiles remaining. There were fewer voices on the radio now, calling out attacks and requests for aid.

I said, "We get back in the fight."

I dropped the nose to recover some energy before pulling back on the stick and throttling to afterburner, vaulting for the heavens on twin rocket blasts like a reborn god and reaching thirty-five thousand feet in less than a minute. From this lofty height, I inverted to survey the battlefield.

Jet fighters chased each other across the sky like a cloud of angry knots among a tangle of disintegrating smoke trails. Far below, the battle for the beaches around Tainan raged on, most of it now shrouded by a drifting pall of smoke and flashes of ordnance. On the strait, transports fireballed among mushrooming hills of water as the bombers staging from Guam arrived to unleash furious salvos of antiship missiles and turn the PLA's amphibious dreams into a horrific massacre of thousands.

Still in neat tactical formation, *Theodore Roosevelt*'s squadrons burst into the area of operations from the south, engaging straggling fighters and shooting antiship missiles amid streams of tracers and SAMs reaching up from some of the ships.

I finally had a moment to feel something, and it came all at once in a surging flood, relief and terror and even some regret, but my overarching emotion was primitive exaltation not only at my own survival but at the extermination of my enemies. My blood sang an ancient song older than Achilles and Hector, as old as Cain. I felt invincible, armed and armored by wrath. I was Thor at Ragnarök, clutching thunderbolts in my fists on the roof of the world.

For the first time during this war, I felt like the hero of my childhood imagination, but I now learned that a hero doesn't always fight for survival or victory or comrades or love or hate, no, in the heat of combat sometimes he reverts to a predatory beast and fights for the purity of fighting, and anything else is just a story waiting to be written later, when others sum up one's deeds and labels him a hero for them.

I spotted another Firebird and swooped in for the kill.

SIXTEEN

War is like a drug, destructive but addictive. It even has a hangover.

Independence cruised five hundred miles west of Pearl Harbor, where it would receive repairs, resupply, and replacements before returning to the theater. The Taiwan War, however, appeared to be done. Aside from sporadic missile strikes and the occasional sinking of a cargo ship, the PRC no longer presented a direct threat to Taiwan, which cautiously celebrated its hard-won independence.

America had scored its own victory, proving itself as the preeminent superpower and the Pacific as its bathtub. China had sacrificed its South China Sea artificial islands, a sizable chunk of its navy and air force, and many of its missiles. The PRC stubbornly refused to recognize Taiwan as a sovereign nation, however, so we'd finish the remainder of our tour taking part in a multinational blockade.

After a brief victory celebration, Mother's routines ground on as the exhausted crew brought her back to port. Among the air wing, which had suffered over fifty percent losses among its strike fighters, there was more shock than jubilation. The ready rooms were quieter, emptier spaces. As for me, I volunteered for any job that needed doing so I could sustain my adrenaline and avoid processing a ton of shit.

Pepsi Man and Duke had joined Snoopy, Dangle, and Track on eternal CAP.

When I wasn't working, I returned to my stateroom to stare at the empty racks, which is where Kyra found me on the eve of steaming into Pearl Harbor.

"Hey," she said. "How are you?"

"Spring loaded," I answered mechanically.

She sat next to me and patted my hand. "We did good."

"Yeah." We did better than good. My first deployment had been an incredible adventure. I'd learned under fire who I really was and what I was made of. I'd shot down four enemy planes in combat, one shy of becoming a fighter ace.

Without my comrades, though, it felt hollow. I'd fought hard to fill a hole in myself, only to trade it for an even bigger, deeper one.

"I have some news," she said. "Tiger says I can serve out my last few weeks in San Diego. I'm leaving the Boat. I'm going home."

"Oh." I'd truly be alone. A month later, I'd be the one leaving as the deployment ended, and after refitting, these racks would be filled with fresh aviators eager to write their own stories.

"I don't want anything to change." I blurted without thinking, "I'm scared, Kyra."

And there it was. Who I really was at the core. What I was made of. Who I'd always been, no matter how bad I'd once wanted to be somebody else.

A boy craving love, recognition, a home.

"Of course you are," she said as if this were the most natural thing in the world. "You're a good man, Jack. Never try to be anything but who you are."

Then she leaned in to deliver a long, deep, and tender kiss.

The dam finally broke, and our kiss became devouring and biting as we attacked each other in a whirlwind of peeling flight suits and groping hands and animal funk. She straddled my lap, and I entered her with a fierce cry of primal need. This was as it should be, a physical union that mirrored the pairing of our souls in the air.

Far beyond lust or love or partnership, we celebrated life the best way humans know how. We'd faced the elephant, and we were alive, it was that simple.

I wanted to hold onto the moment, but everything ends, and then she was gone, and I was alone again.

"Make sure you look me up," was the last thing she said before she left for good.

"Then hold onto this for me," was the last thing I said, giving her my Academy ring for safekeeping, my only possession that had any real value. It was a crazy impulse and corny as hell but as good as a vow that I'd come home to her.

I don't remember much about my lonely liberty in Honolulu. I shared the cost of a hotel suite with several other guys in my squadron, and while they chased giggling ladies in varying states of undress in and out of the rooms, I played the grouch, stuck to myself, missed Kyra, and tried to decompress and unwind using a special lubricant called bourbon. I wasn't exactly pleasant to be around.

I returned to *Independence* to discover our deployment was extended four months on account there was a war on, and my stateroom had filled with replacement aviators. These numbered three bright-eyed nuggets, whom I found irritating because they reminded me of myself, along with two more experienced know-it-alls eager to teach me what I didn't know about the art of flying, including what I didn't know I didn't know.

They all had one thing in common, which was they were going to kick Comrade Wang's ass up and down the Pacific until he saluted hotdogs and apple pie. Tom, my new WSO, meanwhile, discovered I'd fought in every major battle of the war and was a bonafide ace. He took to following me around imitating me, though I didn't care about impressing anybody, not anymore.

The new carrier qualifications completed, we sailed west to join the blockade. The war's next phase had begun: peace talks covering Taiwan and the South China Sea while the allied navies strangled Chinese trade in a campaign designed to squeeze concessions from the People's Republic.

Lieutenant Danby's daily briefings informed us Taiwan was a mess, Russia was rattling its saber, deadlock gripped the United Nations Security Council, America now suffered its own deep recession, and economic ruin and instability racked the PRC.

Speculation abounded about when the Taiwan War would officially end, or if this would turn out to be just the first Sino-American War, and whether all the fighting had merely been the first skirmish of World War Three.

The big, big question on everybody's mind was what was going on in China: who was in charge, and what they might do with the country's nukes.

I didn't think about it all that much. I didn't care. I was too busy trying to figure out why the hell my comrades had died for this mess. For a month, I flew sorties as part of the blockade, counting the days until I could see Kyra again while emailing and calling her on the satphone whenever I had the chance.

"It's not the same without you," I said during one of these calls.

"Be careful," she warned. "This is the part where we lose people because they get sloppy. You'd better stay sharp."

The phone grew slick in my sweating grip. "Sixty-eight days and a wakeup, and I'll be back in San Diego. I'll fly straight up to you."

"I'll be waiting."

"You're being careful too, I hope." I constantly worried about her given the horrible backlash against Chinese-Americans back home.

"I'm *fine*, Jack. Honestly." Her tone brightened as we switched topic from the war to what we'd do together afterwards. "So where are we going again?"

Every time we talked, our future date grew bigger and more extravagant until I forgot the war for a while and lost myself in the fantasy we'd created.

"I have to go," I said with regret after we'd fully fleshed out incorporating a hot air balloon ride. "Duty calls."

"What's it like on the roof?"

"Squalls everywhere, heavy seas, rolling deck. Hooray." I sighed at the prospect of facing it again. "I need a rest."

"I know," she said, her voice smooth as ice cream before snapping, "Now stop moping and get over yourself. You'd better not be getting sloppy."

"I'm not, I swear—"

"The new guys are looking to you to help them get home too."

"Yeah, I guess I—"

"So do your job like a goddamn pro, nugget."

Gripping the phone, I stiffened my spine. "Aye, aye, ma'am."

"I'm serious." Kyra's tone softened again. "Come home to me, Jack."

Minutes later, I left the bank of satphones and mounted the ladders back to my level to grab some quick chow at the Dirty Shirt before my patrol. I made the journey with a spring in my step, missing Kyra something terrible but otherwise feeling clear-headed for the first time in weeks.

The war was what it was. The past could be interpreted later. I'd survived every battle, but I had to stay on my game to make sure I survived the war. Many of my squadron mates weren't the same guys I'd set sail with, but they were still counting on me, just as I was counting on them. They were still my tribe.

In the Dirty Shirt, I spotted Tom, my WSO, wrestling to keep his tray in front of him as the deck pitched on heavy seas. I grabbed some chow and joined him. He was likable enough, good-natured about the minor hazing and always trying hard.

"You've done this before lots of times, right?" he asked me. He was not looking forward to flying in this weather.

"Don't worry," I told him.

Tom turned green. "Kind of scary, though. We'll be landing after dark."

"I've done it enough times. We'll be fine." After surviving air-to-air missiles, I simply didn't believe I would die now in a mundane accident.

"Yeah," Tom said with visible relief at my confidence. "We got this."

We bussed our trays and headed to the ready room

and on into the paraloft to gear up. Athena was our flight lead, and she led us up to the flight deck.

Around us, the Pacific roared and spat under a gray sky like a vast, melancholic god that took no heed of the tiny gnats riding its flood, though its emanations spoke directly to the sparks of their souls. Primordial forces grated their eternal cadence like a monk's chant, inviting me into endless reflection and the chance to become lost with the promise of finding some great truth.

Already damp with misting rain, I paused a moment in awe at the sea's power when Tom tripped over a tie-down chain and face-planted on the deck.

I stared at him. "You all right?"

A bloody nose, embarrassed grin, thumbs-up. "Yeah, Beaver! I'm good!"

I snorted. "Yeah, you look it."

We found our jet, the one with JACK KNAPP stenciled on its side, now decorated with five painted silhouettes of Chinese fighters. We climbed in, warmed up, and taxied to the catapult to await launch.

Surrounded by gray, I gasped as an awful premonition arrived like a surprise thunderbolt.

Then it was gone, leaving me filled with foreboding.

No time to think about it. On the flight deck, the airmen waited for me to signal that I was ready to launch.

I muttered a quick prayer as I delivered my salute.

The catapult fired. Colossal forces shoved my jet off the hard deck and into the unknown. Then I was airborne, racing to catch up to Athena and attach myself to her wing. Together, we vectored toward the first waypoint.

I said over the intercom, "Get ready for a long, boring flight, Tom."

"Maybe we'll find a cargo ship running the blockade," he said. "Maybe even a convoy with a ship that wants to take a pot shot at us. We'll end up—"

I snorted. "You're desperate, brother."

The WSO sighed. *Independence* had faced off against a peer competitor in a sharp, bloody war with one nation and entire seas as the stakes, and emerged victorious. Books and songs would be written about this war, and the aviators who'd fought it had earned stories they'd trade on for the rest of their careers.

Tom had finally made it to the party, only to find himself assigned to clean up the mess.

"Listen," I said. "This is the job. You're doing your part."

"I guess," he moped.

"Right now, my idea of winning is getting home in two months."

Tom said nothing. For an hour, we surfed the soupy sky, flying in and out of squalls that lumbered over the Pacific like Lovecraftian entities.

As I suspected, the patrol passed without incident, and the only major battle I fought was against boredom.

"Tally one boat," Athena radioed.

We were skirting a chain of tiny islands, and she'd discovered a fishing boat that had sought the safety of a cove. We'd check it out.

A burst of light winked below us. My console let out an electrifying cry.

"Hey!" Tom yelled in my ear. "SAM launch!"

In war, you always expect the sucker punch. It looms over you like the Sword of Damocles, and it goes by many terrible names like Shit Happens and The Suck. This cruel god can be kept at bay—using cultivated superstition and a sense of karma built on wishful thinking—but never appeased.

Today was my turn.

Athena popped onto the radio. "Tally launch, five o'clock low!"

Somebody on the fishing boat had taken a shot at us with a handheld, shoulder-fired launcher. We broke left and right, and I ping-ponged in a series of turns while Tom, to his credit, dumped flares for all he was worth.

"Defending!" I gasped.

"Second launch," Athena shot back. "Two SAMs in the air!"

"Do you see it?" Tom asked.

"Negative," I grunted as I continued to twist the jet. "Find it!"

"The first is tracking us. Make that both! Break left and pull hard, hard!"

I did as I was told and ended up nearly inverted, which revealed a spark racing toward me in the thickening dusk. Hicking at the mounting G forces, I twisted again and kept the heat-seeker on my beam until hauling on the control stick and throttling back.

The missile arced past.

"Yeah!" Tom whooped. "One down!"

I jerked my head, searching for the other one. My control stick turned gluey as I leveled out. Not good. Not good at all. I was wallowing now. "What's our speed?"

"Nine-five knots!"

Not enough. I dropped my nose to regain energy, but I was running out of time.

"Break left, Beaver," Athena called out on the radio. "Pull hard!"

I gave the stick all I had in a hail-Mary effort while Tom blew another round of flares, but my jet had bled off the energy it needed for further high-G acrobatics.

The Chinese missile pivoted midair into a sharp, unnatural turn.

And flashed straight behind us.

Oh, shit—

The missile exploded in a heart-stopping boom and blinding flash of light. The jet trembled and lurched as a cloud of high-velocity shrapnel punched through the fuselage and my left wing.

Then a secondary, internal explosion rolled a wall of force that flattened against my back with a jarring thud. Something cracked off my helmet.

In a daze, I gaped at my panel as it lit up with warning indicators. The HUD shuddered and warbled and blinked on and off. Air whistled through the cracked canopy, sending smoke swirling around the bubble.

A fishing boat, I seethed in rage. *A goddamn fishing boat!*

"Flight controls," Bitching Betty twanged. "Engine fire left."

"We're hit!" I called out on the radio. "Mayday, mayday, mayday!"

No answer as I shut down engine one. Either Athena had her own problems, or my radio was toast. The jet rattled around me, and gremlins seemed to be going to town in the back with sledgehammers.

I fought with the stick as I tried to keep control.

"Tom," I yelled over my shoulder. "Tom, can you hear me?"

Nothing.

"Tom. Tom! Say something, goddammit!"

Only the piercing whistle of the wind.

The throttles stopped working. My stick stopped responding.

"I'm dead stick!" I radioed. "Shit! Mayday—"

"Engine fire right," Bitching Betty said. The alarm whooped again. "APU fire."

I shut down engine two and the APU, but the canopy continue to fill with smoke and blazing heat. I worked through the emergency procedures mechanically, refusing to face what I already knew, which was it was hopeless.

The HUD flashed and died.

"Um," I said.

As the last of my lift bled away, the fuselage trembled, ready to surrender to gravity's call. I was out of options and now had mere seconds before my dead Rhino buffeted into a corkscrew that would end in my certain death.

Knowing this, a strange calm washed over me.

I contorted my neck and torso as far as I could to see how Tom was doing.

Parts of him were everywhere.

"I'm sorry, brother. I'm so sorry." Swallowing bile, I added into the radio, "Tom Myers is KIA. I'm ejecting. I'm—I'm punching out."

I didn't want to do this. I wanted to stay right here forever.

Instead, I reached between my thighs to yank the

ejection handle with both hands, offering another hail Mary in the hopes the system hadn't been damaged and would now work.

Forced air jerked and tightened the straps, hauling me back and clamping me tight. The canopy popped away and disappeared.

I gaped up at gray sky as the whistle of wind became a deafening, blasting roar.

Okay, hang on, I thought. *Just wait a minute, wait, no, WAIT—*

My seat shot up the short rail, and I burst from the plane in a nauseating, terrifying lunge straight into the high-speed slipstream, too breathless to scream.

Nothing around me but air and space. Up and up I went in dizzying ascent, shooting a hundred fifty feet over my Rhino before the rocket motor burned out. For a single endless, horrible, breathless second, I hung weightless above the world.

Then gravity reversed and sucked me down.

The drogue chute deployed. A moment later, the main chute opened with a sharp shock and arrested my freefall to the sea, jerking my harness upward with crushing force straight into my chest and back and nuts.

Every bit of breath I still had in my lungs flew out of me in a choking gasp. Below me, my Rhino struck the water with a mighty splash and disappeared in luminescent foam.

The air filled with aerosol roar as a Super Hornet flitted in the distance. Athena! She was still in action. A missile streaked away from her jet toward the cove. The boat disappeared in a flash followed moments later by a thunderous crash and a fireball.

I'd taken my sucker punch. Athena was taking her

vengeance.

"Yes," I growled with pure hatred. "That's for Tom."

Now was a good time to try to contact her. I let go the risers and reached for my handheld radio.

It wasn't there.

The ejection had been so violent, it'd ripped open and emptied several of my pockets. Which meant I was seriously screwed.

Without the radio, it would be very hard to find me. I had two flares to throw, and that was it. My main hope was Athena had spotted my chute and marked my posit.

Falling, falling on the salty wind—

The sea grew louder. I struck the dark water with a sharp gasp, and after that, my memories now are just a kaleidoscope of impressions. Freezing water, bobbing and sputtering on the waves, the roar of the sea, me howling though nobody could hear. Athena buzzed the sky overhead before disappearing into the dark.

Leaving me alone, horribly alone.

Survive, I thought as I struggled on the sea for what seemed like hours. *Survive so you can go home.*

Then a searchlight popped on above the pronounced bow wake of an approaching boat, lighting up the sea like a miniature sun.

SEVENTEEN

What goes up must come down. It's a rule of flying.

Air has weight, and the movement of its molecules creates pressure. A plane's wings are designed such that air flowing over the wing moves faster, which decreases pressure relative to the air under the wing. The difference in pressure creates a force that pushes the wing up into the air.

So the wings make the plane go up, but it is the engines that provide thrust, which in turn generates airflow and moves the plane forward. Because of gravity, an object must be lightweight and fast enough to gain lift.

Once airborne, the aviator uses the stick and throttles to control flight. He or she raises the aileron on one wing and lowers the other to roll the plane left or right. Turns the rudder side to side to make the plane yaw left or right. Adjusts the elevators on the tail to raise or lower the nose's pitch, which makes the plane climb or plunge. Opens or closes the throttles to control thrust.

While this mechanical process gives us the freedom of flight, it is the result of conflict. Lift fighting gravity. Thrust fighting drag. Newton's Laws of Motion producing their own dialectic oppositions and resulting truths.

When a jet approaches the speed of sound, air waves compress around the front of the nose. With enough thrust, the jet breaks through this shockwave to go supersonic, producing a thunderous, victorious boom.

The miracle of flight is the result of ordinary physics, but that does not make it any less miraculous. Starting as a stone, you rise like a feather to join the sport of angels. The horizon drops to expose the world as vast and then small again. Your soul's wings unfurl as you detach from worldly concerns. You surf the winds and clouds and sunlight, living an act of faith and escape, truly living in the moment having found a pure place where there is no story, only you in motion.

Back on the earth, you'll forever keep one eye turned up, forever be homesick to return to the air, forever recall the stark emotional landscape of flight. Even now, a part of me is flying over the Pacific at night, alone with Kyra and my deepening thoughts, the kind of solitude that requires courage and where you feel like you're meeting the real you for the first time. In my mind's eye, the clouds break as I climb through the tops, and billions of stars spill overhead like a revelation of Heaven.

What goes up must come down.

And what comes down will long to return.

EIGHTEEN

Beijing is a sprawling mess of a city.

Two days after the People's Militia fishing boat dragged me out of the water, I found myself being driven from an airfield to Qincheng Prison in a black government van with tinted windows. Manacled by my ankle to a bench in the back, I had just enough leeway to gaze out at the capital of my enemy.

The multilane road swarmed with honking drivers and scooters all vying for the same inch of space like a maniac experiment in automobile Darwinism. China appeared to value harmony but not sensible traffic laws. Apartment complexes loomed against the road until disappearing in a brown polluted haze. Bright yellow propaganda posters seemed to be plastered everywhere, depicting stout and smiling PLA soldiers and zooming jets under shining suns. I recognized the outline of Taiwan on plenty of them.

It all looked like an ugly, soul-crushing dystopia, but a part of me enjoyed it. I'd finally gotten my wish to visit a foreign country.

I turned to my guards, who sat stony-faced on the opposite bench. "Will we drive past the Forbidden City?"

The three men all wore black business suits and ties, two of them built like bears with fists clenched on their knees, the third reading *The People's Daily*. I sensed the latter was in charge. I know a senior officer when I see one.

In response to my query, the two big men stared

at me as if contemplating casual violence. The officer turned the page in his newspaper.

"They do not speak English," he said. "And no, we will not. Great sadness."

The man was you, Deputy Bureau Chief Zhang, though I didn't yet know you were my case officer.

"Does it all look like this?"

This seemed to amuse you. "Ancient Ming tombs are near Qincheng. Astounding history. Quite dramatic. But they are for the People, not war criminals."

"What? I'm not a war criminal."

You shrugged. "Do stupid things, and tragedy befalls you."

We finally left Beijing's clogged arteries and entered a valley devoid of traffic in particular and human life in general. The van drove through a pagoda gate, the most exotic architecture I'd seen since the airport, and discharged us in front of a small one-story building near the dark and sprawling prison, beyond which a mountain loomed with equally foreboding majesty. I climbed out slowly and carefully due to my manacles and the beating the militiamen had given me.

Endless paperwork awaited, after which I officially became a prisoner.

"Welcome to Qincheng Prison, Prisoner 2299," you said.

"It's great to be here," I deadpanned, rubbing at one of my bruises.

You gave me one of your patented smug almost-smiles I'd become familiar with during our interrogations. "Here—how you say in America?—anything you say can and will be used against you. Best be as silent as forgotten memory." You smiled. "At least until I begin my questioning."

After surrendering my name, I handed over my final meager possessions, allowed to keep only my shoes but not my shoelaces. I was given black overalls, plastic utensils, toothbrush and soap, a large enamel water mug. A barber shaved my head to crisp stubble.

Nobody seemed to speak English, barking at me in Chinese and gesturing or kicking me. In this manner, I figured out what I was supposed to do and did it.

The first words I learned in your language were, "Yes, Warden."

All of it was designed to subjugate me and destroy my identity, but honestly, I'd done much of it before when I joined the Navy. I'd been ordered around my entire life and often could fit everything I owned in a sea bag. Which isn't to say I felt anything other than impending doom and more immediate despair. A never-ending plebe summer awaited me. My future promised an endless, miserable suck.

The prison's interior appeared shabby, its dank halls gray and peeling and teeming with a ridiculous number of guards and administrators, all standing around smoking with vacant stares or striding on vital errands for the Party. The cells had green doors. Strange piping twisted out of the floor and disappeared back in the ceiling. Daylight illuminated the corridor though dirty skylights.

It's about what you'd expect for a Club Fed. A shithole.

And judging by how many cells appeared to be occupied, business was currently booming.

At the time, I had no idea just how bad it would end up being. The beatings started soon after, on and off until the warden came and took me to the red interrogation room with its yellow Maoist quotes on the walls.

This is when heaven shined upon me with the great fortune of meeting you formally, Deputy Bureau Chief Zhang. Remember that day? You may recall we didn't start off as the dear, bosom buddies we are now.

"Prisoner 2299, now you may speak," you said. "You will state your name and rank for the record."

"Jack Knapp, Lieutenant, junior-grade, United States Navy."

At the desk next to you, your geeky minion recorded everything I said on camera.

"Why did you destroy the People's hospital ship?" You weren't wasting time and had decided to start right in with the bullshit.

I blinked. This was news to me. "Hospital ship?"

"Why did you murder China's sons and daughters?"

Because they were shooting at me, I wanted to say but held back. "I didn't destroy any hospital ship."

You sat back in disgust and lit one of your expensive cigarettes. "We will start at foolish beginnings. You were aboard *Independence*."

"If you say so."

"Which America sent to China's waters to interfere in an internal security operation. World policeman! What if we parked carriers off Los Angeles? What if we built bases in Mexico, Canada, Cuba, Greenland?"

"I guess we wouldn't invade one of them?"

Wrong answer.

"We are a great power now! The American century is over!"

And that's the crux of it, comrade. You resent America's power not because of how it's used but because you don't have it. You criticize American bullying because you want to be the bully.

This wasn't a debate I was allowed to win, so I struck a reasonable tone. "I don't know what you want to hear. The fact is we do have those carriers and bases. I don't make the policy about how they're used. I can say, though, when you attack one of our allies, it's very likely we're going to respond in some way."

You stabbed out your cigarette in an ashtray. "We will bury you."

I flinched, as whether you meant my country or me personally, it wasn't good, and it sounded like a promise. "You really hate us, don't you?"

"Self-determination for Asia cultivates necessary passion and zeal. The West is like a hollow egg. You have no spirit. Addicted to television and cheap electronics and led by maniac leaders. You treat other nations like lapdogs. You think you rule the world." You squinted at me. "What was China's greatest mistake?"

"That's above my pay grade, sir." This had to be a trick question.

You pointedly glanced at the guards and then back at me. "Indulge me."

"You lied to yourselves."

You scowled. "Explain this statement."

"You told yourselves a lot of things and believed that as long as you said them, they would be true. That's how you lost the war. It's why you can never win."

"Your thinking again is incorrect," you said.

I shrugged. It didn't matter what my thinking was. I was just happy you didn't call on the guards. "Like I said, I'm just an aviator."

"China did not lose the war," you lectured. "China only lose the battle. The Party does not make mistakes. There will be peace, trade, and talk again while we prepare. Next battle will be fought with computer viruses, drones, directed microwave and laser energy, kinetic space weapons, Twitter. This is how we will win the last fight."

You explained the future of warfare. A vast shield of missile-armed drones stretching from the troposphere all the way up to the exosphere. Quantum supercomputer networks impervious to cyberattack. Constant assault by computer viruses that disable and ensnarl command and control networks. Satellite killers. Seafaring magnetic rail guns. Directed microwave beams that fried planes and ships. Wave after wave of missiles launched by land, air, sea, and space. Lasers that would burn warships and carriers from space. Tungsten rods—*rods from God*—dropped from space with enough energy to destroy cities without nuclear fallout. Massive disinformation campaigns on social media designed to foment dissent and division.

Next time, China would use it all and plan for a two-front war.

I believed you. These technologies aren't perfect, would be hard to coordinate and put to good effect, and will take years to fully develop, but if nothing else, China is a patient nation and seems to understand the new arms race.

In the future described to me, wars will be won by nations holding the ultimate high ground, wars that will be fought in orbit, in computer code, and across the electromagnetic spectrum. Weaponry that would make fighter planes, and possibly even navies, unnecessary.

Frankly, I found it both believable and terrifying. We'd already used and encountered the ancestors of some of these weapons during the Taiwan War. But the biggest bummer is my chosen profession might soon be obsolete.

Whether the American century is coming to a close, the romantic century of fighter pilots winning wars may soon enter its own twilight.

NINETEEN

Day after day, my trial before the Tribunal of the Special Court ground on in pointless People's theater, as the prosecutors scolded, witnesses denounced, and the spectators in the gallery dutifully murmured in shock. Like a hapless character in a Franz Kafka novel, I was stuck in an endless trial conducted in a language I didn't understand and with my very life on the line.

Still, it was better than Qincheng Prison. Theater, indeed. It was *One Thousand and One Nights* again, keeping me alive, only this time they were telling the stories.

For the final act, they rolled a series of digital images of young PLA soldiers. Apparently, these were the men on the hospital ship I'd supposedly sunk. Next came pictures of doctors and nurses on the same ship, all of whom had lost their lives. Finally, they showed a picture of the ship itself, which my lawyer told me during a recess was taken moments before I sank it with an antiship missile.

"It is better to see for yourself than to hear it from others," he added, quoting some local proverb about seeing being believing.

"Aren't you supposed to be my defense lawyer?" A question I'd asked many times before.

"If you do not want people to know what you have done, better not to do it."

"If this were a *real* trial—"

He shouted something at the stony-faced bailiffs, and they returned me to the dock before snapping to attention behind me.

Court resumed with another round of witnesses wailing about the horror of the attack. The judges arrayed on the benches scowled over their glasses. I realized the prosecutor was yelling at me, which wasn't new, but he kept repeating the same words over and over.

My lawyer translated, "He wants to know how you feel knowing you destroyed the People's hospital ship."

I stared back at him. "I'm allowed to say something?"

"Answer the question!"

"I didn't—" I stood with an exasperated growl to address the court. I'd rehearsed a dozen lengthy, beautiful speeches for this very moment, but now that it had arrived, I was stuck arguing basic facts. "First off, I fought over Taiwan, not the Strait, so I didn't shoot any ships that day. Second, for God's sake, just look at the bow wakes! In the photo of the ship, you can see a bow wake. The ships behind it are pointed in the same direction, and they also have a bow wake."

All I got was blank stares, so I went on, "The hospital ship wasn't marked as one, and it was carrying troops *to* Taiwan, not wounded *from*—"

Slapping his hand against his table, the prosecutor howled a rapid string of Mandarin in my direction. The gallery joined in the tirade. I turned to the judges expecting them to retake control of their courtroom, but many of them stood to scream at me as well.

At last, a wizened old judge crashed his gavel to restore order and adjourn. The frenzied People had had enough theater for one day.

As the bailiffs opened the dock to return me to Qincheng, I called to my lawyer, "So the judge declared me innocent, and I'm free to go?"

"You are guilty as a thief," he said. "And the judges will rule as such." He offered me a gloating smile. "Great happiness."

I pointed at him, a gesture the Chinese find extremely rude. "You're a great lawyer."

The bailiffs manacled me before marching me out the door through a sea of hateful glares.

You, Deputy Bureau Chief Zhang, waited for me in the prison truck.

"A most interesting defense," you said.

I'd learned to keep things cordial between us, but the trial was driving me insane by this point. "God, no wonder we won the war. You can't even run a convincing show trial."

You chuckled as the truck rumbled back toward the prison. "There were no other ships in the photograph. Only one bow wake."

"Maybe you should Photoshop me into the photo while you're at it, killing everybody with my bare hands."

You found this even more amusing. "No need to be hysterical. I am worried about your state of mind. Prison is not for weak psyche. In a stunning turn, your fantastical insistence you saw more than one ship caused great distress to your case today. Same with persistent delusion you won the war."

I wondered if Kafka ever thought about writing a novel about a system of government designed for the single purpose of gaslighting. Orwell had, creating a society in which if the Party held up four fingers and told you there were five, and you were only considered loyal—and apt to live very long—if you enthusiastically agreed.

"How do you keep all the bullshit in your head, Deputy Bureau Chief?"

"Self-preservation," you answered without batting an eye. "It is my duty to teach you this skill. Our glorious trial achieved its purpose and will soon be over. For weeks, you write a lunatic story. Now you must give a true confession."

"I told you the truth," I said. "Just not what you wanted to hear."

"Your truth, my truth—none of it matters. Only the Party's truth matters. Here is shining truth: Your confession will cultivate unity, and the Party's righteous anger may be soothed as stability is restored. You can end war between our countries, make us good friends again. Do you understand? You can *stop* the war. I have been patient long enough. You will confess." You gazed at me with a little regret. "If you do not..." The speech ended with a shrug. "Tomorrow, the verdict will come."

The penalty for the worst criminals in China is death by firing squad.

"Your government is trying to bring you home," you tried again. "They make demands and threats. If you confess, we may even send you back to America. Certainly, they will understand your confession was coerced."

Sick of all the games and lies, I said nothing, though I was pleased to hear my government was working to get me out of here. My first spark of real hope.

The van passed the Qincheng Prison's pagoda gate and parked. Still manacled, I hobbled toward the building between my guards.

"I know you will make a righteous decision for peace," you called after me.

Back in my blank cell with its bunk and ancient typewriter, I contemplated my options. If the trial is truly going to end tomorrow, I'm out of time. I considered again how to finish my story. What its moral will be.

I'd fought tooth and nail to survive, and I want to survive now. I want to live. I want to get out of this nightmarish place. I want to go home.

Whatever I confess, the Navy would know it was coerced, and I might be forgiven. I might be able to return to duty. I might be able to fly again. I could finally get to know Kyra outside of the Navy.

I would be free.

All I have to do is betray myself, the truth, and both the dead and the living.

And so… No, I just can't do it.

How could I go home if I did? How could I live with myself?

I *won't* do it.

I thought I'd become a hero after I'd shot down Chinese planes. Since then, I've come to understand a real hero gives, not takes. A hero being one who sacrifices for something greater than himself.

I've already sacrificed everything. Now I must make one more sacrifice, this time for truth and my comrades.

I won't betray what I know is real for a made-up story, and more important, I won't betray the friends I lost and those comrades who are still fighting. Maybe if I tell your story, comrade, it'll end the war, or maybe it'll help start the next war.

Either way, it's not worth it to dishonor those I served with.

It's not worth even my life. I'd fought alongside them and I'd fought for them, and that obligation never stops.

So allow me to offer this as my hearty confession:

Go fuck yourself, comrade.

You'll be back soon for my final pages, so I'm going to bring my opus in for a landing and wait for what may be the last LSO grade I'll ever get. In a short time, I'll be getting a bullet in the brain, or maybe a lifetime spent rotting within these dismal walls. Nobody knows when the sucker punch is coming. None of us knows how much time we have left.

The important thing is to do the best we can with the time we have, not just for ourselves, but for our stories, and for the people we owe.

I know exactly how I'm going to spend mine. Chair flying in the big blue, a new story of my own making. Sitting at my desk, I'll forget the typewriter and paper and close my eyes to imagine the flight deck. I'll smell the exhaust and salty air and take in the aerosol hum and blasting roars of aircraft. Kyra is in my backseat, making sure my course remains true. Sam Riggs returns my salute, the green shirt touches the deck, the shooter punches the FIRE button, and we slingshot into a bright, clear sky without enemies.

We rapidly climb the ether seeking the upper limits of the troposphere. Breaking the clouds, we find the Gargoyles, both the living and the dead, burning racetracks and aerobatics in the roof of the world. Snoopy and Track and Pepsi Man and Duke and Dangle and Rowdy and all the rest, still alive and doing what they loved before they gave their all for their country.

To my comrades, no matter what tomorrow brings, one way or another, one day, I'll serve with you again.

STATE MEMO

FROM: Minister Li Guofeng, Ministry of State Security
TO: Vice Chairman, Admiral Sheng Xiaofang, Central Military Commission

Honorable and Respected Vice Chairman, Admiral Sheng, elegantly discerned:

The Central Military Commission charged the Ministry of State Security with detainment and cooperation of the People's Prisoner 2299. This prisoner was captured by the People's Militia forces during the PLA's internal security operation to reunify the nation.

The Tribunal of the Special Court delivered a righteous guilty verdict on all charges of alleged war crimes. Despite this triumphant outcome, the prisoner refused to acknowledge or admit to his heinous crimes.

As you know, a sincere confession would have more powerfully communicated to the world the narrative that China was the true victim of conflict waged by a foreign aggressor. The enclosed document includes statements written by the prisoner, all of it sensational and therapeutic, and none of it correct in its thinking.

Deputy Bureau Chief Zhang's regrettable failure to achieve the most fruitful level of prisoner cooperation will be firmly addressed using patience, education, and healthy discipline. Despite his failure, the trial itself was successful in promoting blessed unity during these turbulent times.

It is now our recommendation that the Ministry of State Security's primary task be recognized as gloriously fulfilled for the People.

This unfetters Prisoner 2299 to become an asset in vital peace negotiations being undertaken by the Ministry of Foreign Affairs with the potential for release to his government. This being based on the Party's position that both countries stand to continue to gain from joyous cooperation and mutual respect.

Respectfully Yours,
Minister Li

WANT MORE?

Thank you for reading!

If you enjoyed *The Aviator*, kindly review the book on Amazon and be sure to check out the sequel, *The Warfighter*.

You might also be interested in Craig's *Crash Dive* series, which depicts submarine warfare in the Pacific during WW2, and *Armor* series, which depicts armored warfare in Europe. These series are available in Kindle eBook (both individually and as a box set), trade paperback, and audiobook formats.

Learn more about Craig's writing at www.CraigDiLouie.com. Be sure to sign up for Craig's mailing list to stay up to date on new releases and receive a link to his interactive submarine adventure, *Fire One*.

And turn the page to read the first chapter of *The Warfighter*!

THE WARFIGHTER

CRAIG DILOUIE

ONE

Let me tell you something about war, Ms. Carter: There is always a sequel.

Humans will return to war again and again regardless of its cost. Because the cost doesn't matter, only who pays and who benefits. Those who benefit most have power and money, while those who pay the most have only love and pride.

A good story gets them all on the same page, so to speak. It was true after the Taiwan War, and it's true now, after the Second Korean War, the twenty-first century's bloodiest and most horrific conflict to date.

These stories are required. Though foreign conflicts have become routine for America, sane people naturally hate it. They don't want to hear their child died in a foreign war that started over American overconfidence, North Korean paranoia, and mutual miscalculations. They need to believe they're fighting World War Two again.

They want a tale of good and evil, and that's where you come in, Lynda—

Sorry, do you mind if I call you Lynda? I think it's great you share the name of the actress who played Wonder Woman in the 1970s. You even look like her. Muscle and boobs, wild mane of black hair, severe and fierce beauty and brains.

I chose you for our interview because you say you support the troops the most. The pilots are all in love with you. From skewering anti-war critics to your caring interviews of military personnel to your unflinching support of the commander in chief, your nightly news hour is staple viewing on the TV in the wardroom.

On Monday night, you will interview me in front of millions. I am being hailed as a hero, the man who saved America from thermonuclear war, though this is just another story. The whole squadron was there when we destroyed that missile, and besides that, I didn't push the button, my weapon systems officer did. The truth is always more complicated.

To prepare for our interview, you asked me to send you some recollections and reminisces, and you will get that and more, probably far more than you bargained for. There's a lot to tell. I am sending you this memoir so that together, maybe we can tell the real story of the Second Korean War—at least my little corner of it, though I ended up at the center of some pretty big events.

Everything I'm going to share with you is off the record and on deep background, but I'm hoping it will educate you about who we are. That it will influence what questions you ask and how you frame your story. I want America to know not only what we fought for, but who fought and what it cost us.

Yes, it's a story about good and evil, but it's also a tale of unimaginable horror. And it's the sum of stories about those who fought it. If you want to know who saved America, it was my squadron, the USS *Independence*, the US Navy.

I have a lot to say and not a lot of time to get it all out, so I should get started. Microphone and recording software, check. Frosty bottle of Sierra Nevada, wonderful. Beautiful view from the beach house of the sun setting over the Pacific, perfect. Like you, Lynda, the vast sea calls me back to Asia, and to the past.

To the war and its nightmare.

I once told a man that war makes a hell of a story, and here's mine.

All of it. The good, the bad, and the monstrous.

ABOUT THE AUTHOR

Craig DiLouie is an author of popular thriller, apocalyptic/horror, and sci-fi/fantasy fiction.

In hundreds of reviews, Craig's novels have been praised for their strong characters, action, and gritty realism. Each book promises an exciting experience with people you'll care about in a world that feels real.

These works have been nominated for major literary awards such as the Bram Stoker Award and Audie Award, translated into multiple languages, and optioned for film. He is a member of the Horror Writers Association, Science Fiction and Fantasy Writers of America, and International Thriller Writers.

Learn more about Craig's writing at www.CraigDiLouie.com. Be sure to sign up for Craig's mailing list to be the first to learn about his new releases.

Other books by Craig:

The Warfighter
Crash Dive Series
Armor Series
The Children of Red Peak
Our War
One of Us
Suffer the Children
The Retreat Series
The Alchemists
The Infection
The Killing Floor
Tooth and Nail

Craig DiLouie

Craig DiLouie's six-episode Crash Dive series chronicles the adventures of Charlie Harrison as he fights the Imperial Japanese Navy during WW2. Gripping, action-packed, authentic, and filled with larger-than-life men of the Greatest Generation, Crash Dive puts you aboard a submarine during the war.

You'll stand alongside Charlie as he proves himself by being decisive in crisis. You'll attack a convoy in a daring night surface attack, emerge in a sea fog to ambush a battle group, and charge the battleship Yamato during the decisive Battle of Leyte Gulf. All the while, you'll live with the crew in the cramped, noisy, and challenging machine that was a diesel-electric submarine.

"Adventure fiction in the grand tradition of the Hornblower series... Crash Dive blew me away."
- John Dixon, author of *Phoenix Island*

Made in United States
North Haven, CT
03 April 2022

17825873R00145